Pet Finders Club

Looking For Lola

by Ben M.

SCHOLASTIC INC.

New York   Toronto   London   Auckland   Sydney
Mexico City   New Delhi   Hong Kong   Buenos Aires

Special thanks to Liss Norton

ISBN 0-439-68885-X

Text copyright © 2004 by Working Partners Limited.
Illustrations copyright © 2004 by Scholastic Inc.

12 11 10 9 8 7 6 5 4 3 2 1   5 6 7 8 9 10/0

Printed in the U.S.A.
First Scholastic printing, March 2005

Chapter One

"See you later, little Bud," Andi Talbot whispered, crouching down to pet her Jack Russell terrier. "Be good for Mom." She truly hated leaving him every morning when she went to school, but at least he'd have her mom around to keep him company today.

A few months ago, Andi and her mom, Judy Talbot, had moved from Florida to Orchard Park, a suburb of Seattle. After using a local Laundromat all that time, Judy Talbot had decided it was time for their own washing machine. She'd taken the day off so it could be delivered that morning.

"I'd better get back, honey," Mrs. Talbot said. "In case the machine arrives early."

"Just think — no more Saturday afternoons at Soak 'n' Suds!"

Her mom smiled. "Tell me about it! A weekend will finally be a weekend!"

Andi kissed her mom. "See you later." She gave Buddy another pat, then ran across the playground to join Larissa, Kelly, and Howard, who she knew from homeroom and science class.

"Hey, guys!" she shouted.

Howard jumped.

"Whoa, Howard," Andi said, surprised that she had startled him.

"Oh, hey, Andi," he said. "Sorry. Larissa's been telling us about the ghost her cousin's friend saw in Tangletree House last night." He ran his fingers through his hair, making it stick out at all angles. "I guess I got a little spooked."

"Andi doesn't look anything like a ghost," Kelly pointed out, switching her cat-print tote bag to her other shoulder. "You need glasses, Howard."

"Who says they saw this ghost?" Andi asked. She didn't believe in stuff like that, but it sounded like a good story. "Larissa's friend's cousin?"

"No, my cousin's friend," Larissa corrected her. "He said he saw a pair of huge glowing eyes staring out at him from a window one night."

Andi laughed. It sounded like something Larissa's cousin's friend had seen in a horror flick.

Kelly squealed. "I bet it's Agnes Delaney!" she said excitedly. "She was murdered in Tangletree House a hundred years ago, or something."

It still sounded phony, but Andi felt the hairs on the back of her neck prickle. "How do you know?"

"It was in the local paper a few weeks back. They ran a story about the house because it's going to be renovated for apartments."

"I read that article, too," Larissa said. "Agnes's nephew murdered her for her money, apparently."

"I bet she's come back from the dead to drive the builders away," Howard said. "She probably doesn't want anyone messing with her house."

"Yeah," Kelly agreed, her gray eyes wide. "I wouldn't want to work there. Too creepy!"

Chen, the last member of their science-class study group, came running over and dropped his camouflage backpack on the ground. "Hey, are you guys talking about Tangletree House?" he asked. "Lonny Kennedy says she heard a ghost wailing in there when she passed by on her way to school this morning."

They all stared at him. A cold chill tingled down Andi's spine. She reminded herself again that she didn't believe in ghosts. But if other people had heard it . . .

"It must be true, then," Howard declared. "I'm gonna go check it out."

Chen laughed. "You wouldn't dare."

"Come with me if you want."

Kelly gave a little shriek. "Don't go near that place!"

Andi noticed her friend Natalie waving to her from across the playground. She ran to join her. "What's all the gossip about?" Natalie asked, flipping her shiny blond hair over her shoulder. As usual, she looked like she had just been to a salon, while Andi felt as though she looked like she'd done ten laps on the track.

"There's a ghost at Tangletree House," Andi explained.

Natalie made a face. "Whatever!"

"I thought that, too," Andi said. "But now Lonny supposedly heard it wailing."

Natalie laughed. "Uh-huh."

"No, listen!" Andi persisted. She told her about Agnes Delaney.

"Tell you what," Natalie suggested, picking a long blond hair off her jacket and letting it blow away. "Let's walk past Tangletree House after school and see if we can meet this ghost. I'll bet we don't!"

"Uh . . . okay." Andi hoped Natalie was right about there being no such things as ghosts.

"What are you two up to?" asked a voice, suddenly.

A red-haired, freckle-faced boy was standing behind them.

"Tristan! I should have known it was you," Natalie said sharply, "creeping up on us like that!"

"Me?" he said indignantly. "Creep?" He flung his arms out as though he'd just finished a song-and-dance number on stage. "Am I the sort of guy who creeps? What do you look so secretive about, anyway?"

"We're going ghost hunting after school," Andi told him. "Want to come?"

Tristan's eyebrows shot up. "Ghost hunting? I thought we hunted for lost animals."

Not long after Andi had moved to Orchard Park, she and Tristan and Natalie had set up the Pet Finders Club, to help people who'd lost their pets.

"Not today," Natalie said. "We're going to Tangletree House after school."

"We're not going inside," Andi added hurriedly. "We're just walking past."

"I can't," Tristan said. "Christine's having two pythons delivered." Tristan often helped out at the local pet store, Paws For Thought, which was owned by his mom's cousin, Christine Wilson. "Do you want to come see them?"

"No way!" Natalie said with a shudder.

Tristan laughed. "What, so snakes are worse than ghosts?"

"A zillion times worse!" Natalie insisted. "It's impossible not to believe in them, for a start!"

"Sit down quickly," called Mr. Dixon as the kids filed into their classroom.

Andi and Natalie saw eyebrows raise across the room. Mr. Dixon was usually much more cheerful than this, so Andi wondered if they were about to be reprimanded for something. Ms. Ashworthy and her class were also in the classroom waiting for them. Tristan was sitting on the far side of the room, near the window.

"Fill up the empty chairs first," Ms. Ashworthy told Mr. Dixon's class. "The rest of you can sit on the floor."

Mr. Dixon finished taking attendance and then addressed the students. "Ms. Ashworthy and I want to speak to all the fifth graders together." He still looked grim.

Andi flashed a quick smile at Tristan as she looked around for an empty chair. He grinned back.

"What's so funny, Tristan Saunders?" demanded Ms. Ashworthy.

"Nothing!" Tristan said hurriedly, turning to face the front again.

The empty chairs were soon taken, so Natalie and Andi sat down on the floor. "This is so going to ruin my skirt," Natalie complained.

"Now," said Ms. Ashworthy, once everyone was settled. "It seems as though the whole school is talking about Tangletree House this morning."

A murmur of excitement swept around the room, which Ms. Ashworthy squashed with a glare down her long nose.

Mr. Dixon looked around sternly. "Nobody is to go to Tangletree House in the hope of proving the legends right or wrong. Construction sites are dangerous places, as I'm sure you all know."

"Anyone who is seen on the site will find themselves in detention for a week," Ms. Ashworthy warned. "So stay away."

Andi glanced at Natalie, who was fiddling with the beads on her skirt. Andi couldn't see her face, but she was willing to bet that Ms. Ashworthy's threats wouldn't be enough to keep Nat away from Tangletree House that afternoon.

Natalie was waiting for Andi when she came out of the locker room after soccer that afternoon. "How did it go?" she called.

"Not bad. I scored two goals, so Mr. Wallace will definitely put me in the game next week!" Andi gave her a high five. "How was chess club?"

Natalie groaned. "I was hopeless. I kept thinking about the ghost. Jordan Maloney beat me twice, and she's never going to let me forget it."

"Sure she will. She's got a brain like a sieve. She forgets her homework or her sneakers at least once a week." Andi paused before asking the question she knew Nat was waiting for. "So, do you still want to go to Tangletree House?"

"You bet!"

"Where is it?" Andi asked.

"On Windrush Drive, on the other side of the park. We can pick up Jet and Buddy on the way."

Natalie lived closest to the school, so they got her black Labrador first. He bounced around her while she tried to clip on his leash. "Calm down!" Natalie pleaded. Jet dragged them along the sidewalk to Andi's house as if he were a sled dog.

"Hi, Mom!" Andi called as she opened the front door. "Did the washing machine come?"

"Yes, thank goodness," Judy Talbot replied, coming into the hall with Buddy at her heels. "I've done three loads already. Oh, hi, Natalie." She patted Jet. "Are you guys going for a walk?"

"Yeah, to the park." Andi dropped her backpack on the hall table and checked the phone to see if the message light was flashing. It could mean another case for the Pet Finders to solve. But there were no messages. *Uh-oh*, thought Andi. *Now we'll really have to go check that house out.* As she grabbed Buddy's leash, she reminded herself for the tenth time that she didn't believe in ghosts.

The park looked beautiful in the early November sunshine. The trees were shades of orange, scarlet, and gold, with some of the leaves falling gently to the ground. As soon as Andi let Buddy off the leash, he tore away from them, then circled around with his mouth open in a wide, doggy grin.

"I wish I could let Jet off," said Natalie, "but I can't trust him to come back when I call."

Andi shivered, remembering the time Jet and Buddy had both gotten lost, and how she'd been convinced she'd never see her dog again.

Buddy leaped up at her, and Andi rubbed her fingers against his tan-and-white fur. "Thank goodness I got you back, boy."

As they climbed the hill toward the woods, Buddy began to bark at something behind them. Andi looked back to see what he'd spotted. A pint-sized dog was edging along a path on the far side of the pond. It was oatmeal-colored and looked just a little taller than Buddy, though it was hard to be sure from this distance.

"What a cute dog!" Andi exclaimed. Instinctively she looked around for the dog's owner. "I wonder who it belongs to."

The dog didn't even glance at them, but disappeared into some shrubs. Immediately, Buddy bounded off after it. "No! Come back, Buddy," Andi called.

Obediently, he stopped, turned, and trotted back, and Andi crouched down to hug him.

"He's so good," Natalie sighed. "Do you see that, Jet? Buddy knows how to behave when he's off his leash."

"I can't see anyone who could be that dog's owner," Andi said thoughtfully. "What if it's lost, and it turns out to be another case for the Pet Finders Club? Maybe we should go catch it."

"We can't go chasing after every loose dog we see," Natalie pointed out. "If we did, there'd be some pretty angry owners around demanding to know why we were grabbing their pets."

"I guess you're right."

"In any case, the dog's owner is probably behind those bushes," Natalie said as they went on. "And we're supposed to be ghost hunting, not dog hunting."

They were nearly into the woods when the little dog came rocketing past them. "No way is that dog out with an owner!" Andi exclaimed. "I think it might really be lost." She held out her hand. "Here! Come on! Good dog."

Again, the dog took no notice. It shot in among the trees and disappeared. "Let's see if we can catch up with it," Andi suggested.

They started to run, but by the time they reached the trees, the dog had vanished.

"It's probably gone home," Natalie puffed, catching up with Andi and leaning against a trunk. "It was wearing a collar, so it must belong to someone."

"Maybe," Andi said. But deep down, she knew she was just looking for an excuse not to go to Tangletree House. Larissa's story had scared her far more than she was going to let Natalie know!

The light was beginning to fade when they emerged on the other side of the woods and headed down Windrush Drive. Soon, they stood in front of a four-story house with a pitched slate roof and windows like sinister beady eyes, silhouetted against the darkening sky. Andi gulped.

It looked like something out of a movie, even without all the stories about ghosts and murdered aunts.

"This is it," Natalie announced. "Tangletree House."

The house was surrounded by a tall chain-link fence with notices warning trespassers to keep out. From where they were, Andi could just make out a row of huge dark holes dug in the ground to the right of the house, bulldozers standing idle above them. Most of the garden had been cleared, but a tangle of overgrown shrubs and briars still grew close to the house's north wall, separating the house from the construction site. The whole area was deserted, and the silence made it even eerier.

"Let's get closer," Natalie suggested. There was a slight tremor in her voice, and Andi glanced at her.

"You nervous?" she asked.

"No. I told you, there's no such thing as ghosts."

They started to walk toward the house. Suddenly, Buddy bounded forward, barking wildly and almost jerking the leash out of Andi's hands. "Stop it, Buddy," she scolded.

But Buddy kept on barking, and then Jet threw back his head and howled.

"What's wrong with them?" Natalie whispered, turning pale.

"P-people say animals are sensitive to the supernatural," Andi stammered. "Maybe they can see something we can't."

Natalie's eyes grew wide with fear. "You don't mean . . . ?"

Andi nodded, her teeth chattering. "The stories about Agnes Delaney's ghost must be true!"

Chapter Two

The next day after school, Andi was doing her home-work at the kitchen table when the phone rang. She jumped up to answer it.

"Hello, is this the Pet Finders Club?" asked a woman's voice.

Andi's heart flipped. "Yes," she replied, hoping she sounded calm and professional. "Can I help you?"

"Oh, I hope so. I've lost a pet."

"Is it an oatmeal-colored terrier cross?" Andi blurted out, remembering the dog she and Natalie had seen at the park the day before. They hadn't noticed it on their way home from Tangletree House last night — but they had both been running so fast, even Natalie would have made the school track team if Coach had been watching them.

The woman seemed surprised. "No, she's a cat. A purebred Russian Blue named Lola."

Andi picked up the pen from the message pad by the phone. "Can you give me your name and address, please?"

"I'm Helen Giacomo. And I live at number five Scayne Place."

Andi scribbled it down. "How long has Lola been missing, Ms. Giacomo?"

"Two days. She must have escaped from my house somehow, and I'm so worried. She's expecting kittens."

Andi's heart went out to her. Ms. Giacomo sounded very upset, and Andi remembered only too clearly how awful she'd felt when she'd lost Buddy. "Don't worry," she said. "We'll find her for you. Can we come to your house to get some more information?"

"Absolutely. I'll be here for the rest of the day."

"I'll just call the other Pet Finders," Andi said, "and we'll be right over. Give us half an hour." She put down the phone, her heart pounding with excitement at the thought of investigating another pet disappearance. Their last case resulted in finding dozens of missing animals from Christine's pet store. This case would be much easier, she thought hopefully. A pregnant cat wasn't likely to have strayed too far, and one single cat would be a lot easier to find than the bunch of gerbils, snakes, and parrots had been.

Tristan was already waiting outside Ms. Giacomo's house when Andi arrived. He was holding a three-ring binder with a shiny red cover. "What do you think?" he asked, holding it up. "I got it from my mom and dad's real estate office. I thought we could keep notes in it."

"Awesome! It looks really official."

Natalie soon came hurrying around the corner. "Sorry I'm late. I couldn't find my cell phone."

"No way." Tristan raised his eyebrows in disbelief. "Do you mean it doesn't come with a built-in satellite location system?"

Natalie made a face at him. Tristan always gave her a hard time about the extravagant accessories she owned. "I found it," she said. "It had slipped down the side of my bed." She pulled it out of her pocket. "Hey! Don't forget this phone helped us solve our last case. If I hadn't been able to take a picture of that house, Fisher and Christine would never have known where we were."

"Okay, okay." Tristan held up his hands. "You don't need to remind me." He and Andi had gotten into a lot of trouble for entering a rundown house where a thief had been hiding out.

A short, plump woman with gray hair answered the door when Natalie rang the bell at 5 Scayne Place. "We're the Pet Finders Club," Tristan introduced them.

"Come in. I'm so glad to see you." She led the way into her living room, where the walls were covered in shiny certificates and awards. A huge, rather gaudy gold trophy stood on the mantelpiece. But there was a pretty silver-gray toy cat draped on the arm of the sofa. Andi stared at it, wondering if it looked like Lola. She stroked it idly, then jumped back, shocked, as it twitched its ears and began to purr. It was real!

"That's Lola's sister, Deena," Ms. Giacomo explained. "She misses Lola almost as much as I do."

The cat glanced up at Andi with mournful green eyes.

"Please sit down," Ms. Giacomo said.

"Do Lola and Deena look alike, Ms. Giacomo?" Andi asked, sitting beside Deena. Photos would be helpful for finding out what the missing cat looked like, but seeing an identical cat would be even better.

"Lola's fur is a little paler and her ears are more pointed. She's smaller, too. Wait, I have a photo here." Ms. Giacomo took a photo out of a drawer and handed it to Andi. Lola was looking straight into the camera. Her tail was curled over her front paws and her ears were pricked up curiously.

"She's lovely!" Andi exclaimed.

"She is," agreed Ms. Giacomo. "And she's very friendly."

"Like my cat, Lucy," Tristan whispered to Andi. "*She* was friendly, too." Lucy had been missing for about three months, since before Andi had moved to Orchard Park.

Andi patted Tristan's arm. She knew he still missed Lucy badly, but there didn't seem much chance of finding her now, after so long. She passed the photo to Natalie.

"What a cute face!" Natalie exclaimed. She handed it to Tristan.

"Can we keep the photo please, Ms. Giacomo?" Andi asked. "We'll need to scan it into my computer when we make posters."

"Of course."

Tristan looked at the photo solemnly, then tucked it inside the front cover of the notebook.

"You told Andi that Lola had escaped from the house. Does that mean you don't usually let her out?" Natalie asked.

"Only when I'm there to watch her. And then she only goes into the yard." Ms. Giacomo smiled sadly. "She loves it out there."

"But she got out on her own this time?" Tristan queried.

"She must have. We had a couple of warm days, and I left the back door open with only the screen door to keep the cats inside."

"When did you first realize she was missing?" Natalie asked.

"It was quite early. I'm always up by six o'clock, and I opened the door at about a quarter to seven." Ms. Giacomo sighed. "I noticed she wasn't here at about seven thirty, but she could have been gone for a while."

Tristan wrote these details in the red binder.

"The yard is fenced all around," Ms. Giacomo continued. "But I guess Lola could have scaled the fence if she'd gotten out of the house without me noticing."

"Can we take a look at the yard?" Andi asked.

"Of course."

They followed Ms. Giacomo out of the living room, across a narrow hall, and into the kitchen. Ms. Giacomo opened the back door and led them into a grassy yard surrounded by a wooden fence about six feet tall. "A cat could get over that in no time, with no one watching," Natalie said in a low voice.

Andi went back into the kitchen to check the screen door. The catch clicked firmly shut when Andi closed it.

"I don't see how she could have gotten out through here," she whispered to Tristan.

"Maybe Ms. Giacomo didn't close it all the way," he replied. "The wind might have blown it open just enough for Lola to squeeze through."

They went back to the living room. Tristan carefully wrote down details about the yard and the screen door in the binder. Andi and Natalie exchanged a grin. Tris could be very serious about the detective stuff — but he had such a curiously good memory, he probably didn't need to write all this down, anyway.

"What does Lola eat?" asked Andi. Tristan and Natalie stared at her in surprise. "We might need to tempt her down from a tree or out of some hiding place," she explained.

"She has a dry food mix," Ms. Giacomo said. "I'll get you some." She disappeared into the kitchen and came back with a plastic bag containing some food. "Here you are." Andi smiled as she took the bag. Ms. Giacomo was giving them a lot of helpful information that could lead them straight to Lola.

Natalie glanced around at the rows of certificates. "It looks like Lola has won a lot of shows. That must mean she's pretty valuable. Do you think she might have been stolen?"

Ms. Giacomo gasped. "Oh, no! Surely not!" She swept Deena into her arms and hugged her tightly. "That would be terrible! Poor Lola!" Her eyes filled with tears. "And the poor kittens!"

"I'm sorry. I didn't mean to upset you," Natalie said hurriedly.

"It's all right. It's not your fault. I get upset all the time since Lola's disappeared." Ms. Giacomo dabbed her eyes with a tissue. "Losing your pet is one of the worst things in the world."

"It is," Tristan agreed. "But I doubt Lola has been stolen. She probably wandered off somewhere. Only a cat expert would know she was worth a lot of money. It's not like someone stealing snakes or lizards. Everyone knows they're worth a bundle."

"Yes, of course." Ms. Giacomo smiled weakly. "Is there anything else you need to know?"

"I don't think so," Natalie said. "You've given us a lot to get started with."

"We'll search around here first," Andi said. "Then, if we don't find Lola, we'll start putting up posters. We'll make flyers, too, and deliver them to every house nearby. Maybe Lola's gotten trapped in a shed or something. We'll ask everyone to check." She smiled at Ms. Giacomo. "Don't worry, we'll find her."

"Oh, I hope so," Ms. Giacomo said. "Thank you for being so helpful."

They said good-bye and made their way slowly along the sidewalk, peering into gardens and under parked cars as they went. Every house on the block was different. Some were large and old with narrow windows and tall chimneys; others were smaller and more modern.

There was no sign of the missing cat anywhere, but if Lola wasn't used to being outside on her own, Andi knew she might have gotten scared and run a long way before looking for somewhere to hide.

A tall pine tree stood at the end of the street where they stopped. "What's that noise?" Natalie asked, stopping right under the tree and clutching Tristan's arm.

"What noise?" said Tristan.

"Something rustling, up in the tree."

They peered up into the branches, listening. Sure enough, there it was again — a scratching noise from above. "It might be Lola!" Natalie whispered excitedly. "Maybe she got stuck."

They gazed up, but the branches were too dense to see what was making the noise. "I'll climb up," Andi said. She grabbed the lowest branch and hauled herself into the tree.

"Are you sure this is a good idea?" Tristan said. "We

don't want to have to take you to the emergency room."

"I'll be fine," Andi said, stretching up for another handhold. The branches were strong enough to bear her weight, and she was a good climber. Soon, she was completely surrounded by pine needles. They blocked out most of the light, and she felt as though she was inside a cool, green cave. She stopped climbing to listen. For a moment, there was no sound but the revving of a distant car engine. Then she heard a tiny scratching directly above her head. She peered up, but there was nothing to see but branches.

"Can you see her, Andi?" Natalie called.

"Not yet." Andi climbed onto the next branch. It was thinner than the last one and it creaked under her weight. She knew she wouldn't be able to go much higher; the branches wouldn't be strong enough to hold her as she neared the top of the tree. She hoped Lola hadn't climbed so high that she was out of reach.

Suddenly, there was a frantic scrambling sound above her head. A moment later, a squirrel scampered past her and darted down the other side of the trunk and into some shrubs around its base.

"Aw! It was only a squirrel!" Andi cried, disappointed.

"There's no way Lola could be up there, then," Tristan

called. "A squirrel would never stay in a tree with a cat. You might as well come down, Andi."

Andi slid down the tree trunk. "What a shame," she said, picking pine needles out of her hair. "I really thought we'd found her."

"Let's keep looking," Natalie said, brushing off Andi's coat. "You are totally going to need to take this to the dry cleaner's."

They turned the corner and found a small diner on the next street. "I wonder if they've seen Lola," Andi said. "When Buddy was lost, a chef gave him a slice of pizza. Remember, Tris?"

"How could I forget? We found out about it right after I'd been stuck in that hedge!"

"You were stuck in a hedge?" Natalie hooted with laughter. "I wish I'd been there to see it."

"I had to pull him out," Andi told her.

"You should have left him there."

Tristan folded his arms, pretending to be offended. "Remind me not to help *you* next time you get in trouble."

"Quit it, you guys. Are you coming in or not?" asked Andi, pushing open the door of the diner.

There were no customers, but a waitress was setting

out knives and forks. "Sorry, we're not open yet," she said. "Can you come back in about half an hour?"

"We're looking for a lost cat," Tristan told her. "We wondered if she's been here." He showed the waitress Lola's picture.

"No, though we had a little dog begging for scraps this morning. She was here yesterday, too."

"A dog?" Andi said.

"Yes, such a cutie! Cream-colored and really friendly."

"Cream-colored like oatmeal?" Natalie inquired. The waitress nodded, and Natalie looked at Andi. "You don't think . . . ?"

"It must be the dog we saw at the park," Andi said. She tore off the corner of a page from Tristan's notebook and, ignoring his indignant look, scribbled her phone number on it. "If you see her again, could you call us, please? We're the Pet Finders Club, and we help people who've lost their pets."

"What dog?" Tristan asked as they went out. "What's all this about? Are you two keeping secrets from ace detective Tristan Saunders?"

"We saw it yesterday," Andi told him. "It seemed to be alone, but we couldn't tell for sure." She wished now that they'd tried harder. She didn't like to think of the poor dog running around, lonely and frightened. "We should keep a look out for that dog, as well as Lola."

"You know what this means," Tristan said excitedly. He grinned at Andi and Natalie. "The Pet Finders Club has two cases under investigation!"

Chapter Three

"What now?" Andi asked when they'd searched all along the next two streets without seeing any sign of Lola.

"We'd better go start on the posters," Natalie suggested. "The sooner we let people know that Lola's missing, the sooner we'll find her."

"First, I want to go back and talk to Ms. Giacomo one more time," Tristan said. "I'm beginning to think Natalie's idea that Lola might have been stolen could be right."

"But who'd steal a cat?" Andi asked. "I mean, she's Ms. Giacomo's *pet*."

"But she's a *valuable* pet," Tristan reminded her. "And a pregnant one, at that. Pedigree kittens sell for a lot of money."

Ms. Giacomo met them at the front door. "Have you found her?"

"Not yet," Andi admitted as they followed her into the living room and sat down. Deena jumped straight onto Tristan's lap and started kneading his leg with her front paws.

"What is it?" Ms. Giacomo asked anxiously, looking around at their solemn faces. "Is there something you're not telling me?"

"No," Andi said as gently as she could. "Not really. But we're wondering about the chance that Lola *has* been stolen."

Ms. Giacomo nodded. "I thought about that some more, too. It's a possibility."

"The thief would have to be someone who knows how valuable Lola is," Tristan pointed out, scratching the side of Deena's head. She rolled over, purring louder than ever, and he tickled her tummy.

"Is there someone in Orchard Park who'd know about Russian Blues?" Natalie asked.

"Well, there's Paul Channing, of course. But there's no way he'd steal Lola. We're practically neighbors — he only lives on the next street — and he breeds Russian Blues, too."

Tristan entered Mr. Channing's name in his notebook, resting it on the arm of the sofa to avoid squashing Deena.

Andi spotted a newspaper clipping pinned to a board over a desk. "It says here that Lola won that trophy in a show in Seattle, and that her show name is Princess Anastasia."

"That's right."

Deena began to chew the corner of Tristan's notebook, so he put his hand over it, and she licked his fingers instead. "Did Mr. Channing enter a cat?" he asked.

"Well, yes. Two actually, but . . . "

"Aha!" Holding Deena back with his left hand, Tristan scribbled in the notebook again. "Did they win prizes?"

"Second and third. But really, I can't imagine . . . " Ms. Giacomo trailed off.

"How did Mr. Channing react when he found out his cats hadn't won?" asked Andi.

Ms. Giacomo was looking rather flustered. "He congratulated me. His cats, Snowdrop of the Steppes and Beauty of Babylon, often come in second or third to Lola. But if you're thinking Paul could be a thief . . . well, he just can't be. I've known him for years."

"Can you think of anyone else who might know that Lola's valuable?" Andi asked. Ms. Giacomo seemed so certain that Mr. Channing couldn't be involved in Lola's disappearance, they were probably following the wrong lead.

Ms. Giacomo shook her head. "Well, not in Orchard Park. But people come to these shows from all over."

"That proves it, then," Tristan whispered to Andi. "If she's been stolen, this Mr. Channing must have done it."

"It doesn't prove anything, Tristan," she hissed back. "First of all, why would Mr. Channing have waited until now to take Lola, when she has beaten his cats so often? Unless he was after the kittens, of course. . . ."

"We've got to make those posters," interrupted Natalie.

"Thanks again for helping me," Ms. Giacomo said as they headed for the door. "If you need to know anything else, just give me a call."

"We will," Andi promised.

They hurried down the driveway. "It's obvious where Lola is," Tristan said as they closed the gate behind them. "Mr. Channing's got her."

"We don't know that," Andi said.

"*I* do. Who stands to gain the most from Lola disappearing?"

"Mr. Channing. Maybe. But that doesn't make him a thief," Andi argued. "Ms. Giacomo doesn't even think he's done it."

"He's the most likely person to have taken her. I bet

he secretly hates Ms. Giacomo because her cat wins more prizes than his. We should go over to his house right now and look around." Tristan shoved the notebook into his backpack, looking very determined.

"We *cannot* break in!" Natalie pointed out. "I'm not about to test the police again after our last case."

Andi cringed at the thought of how recklessly they'd acted while rescuing Christine's stolen animals. "Depending on what he does, he could be at work now, anyway."

Tristan grinned. "Perfect! He might have left a window open."

Andi and Natalie stared at him in disbelief. "You're not suggesting what I think you're suggesting, are you?" Natalie asked. "Even *you* couldn't be dumb enough to want to break into Mr. Channing's house."

"No way!" Andi cried. "We'd get into way too much trouble for something like that. And there's no proof he took Lola. When Paws for Thought was robbed, we suspected a ton of people who had nothing to do with it. We can't make the same mistake this time."

Natalie grabbed Andi's arm. "Come on. Let's go make those posters and leave this nutcase to get arrested on his own."

"Wait!" Tristan called, running after them. "Okay, okay, I don't exactly want to break into his house, but you've got to admit he's a top suspect."

"He's a possibility," Natalie said. "And that's all. Now, are you coming with us, or should we get ready to bail you out of jail?"

"I guess I'll make posters," Tristan muttered. "But you're making a big mistake. Mr. Channing's got Lola, I'm sure of it."

"That's it," Andi said as the last of the flyers came spooling out of the printer. The Pet Finders were crammed into her mom's tiny study, and Buddy was lying on Andi's feet, as he always did when she worked at the computer. Andi picked up a flyer and looked it over with satisfaction. Lola's sweet face gazed back at her.

"Looking for Lola," Andi read out loud. *"Have you seen this cat? Please check sheds and garages."* Her phone numbers were printed at the bottom, as usual.

"How many posters have we printed?" Natalie said.

"Twenty," Andi replied. "And forty flyers."

"It's a waste of time and paper," Tristan grumbled, picking up the pile of posters and flapping them at Andi. "We all know who's got Lola. She'd be back with Ms. Giacomo by now if you'd listened to me."

"If you're so determined to investigate Mr. Channing, why don't you and Andi take some flyers, knock on all the doors on his street, and ask if anyone's seen a lost cat? Then you can see how he reacts when you ask him about Lola."

"Aren't you coming with us?" Andi asked.

Natalie groaned. "I have to go to the dentist!"

"Poor you," Andi sympathized.

Tristan looked much more cheerful. "That's a terrific idea!"

"What? Going to the dentist? I don't think so."

"No, knocking on doors. We might even be able to trick our way into Mr. Channing's house."

"We don't know his address," Andi pointed out.

Tristan reached for the phone book. "It'll be in here." He flicked through the pages. "Channing, Channing . . . Here it is, Channing, P., 19 Windrush Drive."

"Windrush Drive?" Andi echoed. "Isn't that where Tangletree House is?"

"Yep." Tristan shut the phone book with a snap, making Buddy look up.

Andi bent down and patted him. "Let's take Buddy with us. And I don't want to be down there when it starts to get dark."

"Scared of the ghost?" Tristan said. "You're supposed to be the most sensible one of the three of us."

Natalie nudged him crossly with her elbow, and Andi frowned. Being sensible sounded *way* boring!

"Anyhow," Tristan continued, "I passed Tangletree House a few days ago, when I was helping Dean with his paper route, and I didn't see or hear anything weird. Those stories are hoaxes." He looked disappointed, as if ghosts were almost as cool as snakes.

"Well, are we going, or what?" Andi cut in. She didn't want to think about Tangletree House. Buddy and Jet's reaction the other night had been pretty scary.

"Sure." Tristan jumped up. "The sooner, the better, actually. My mom was complaining this morning that she never sees me these days, so I promised I'd be home early."

"She complained about never seeing you?" Natalie said, astonished. "Is she crazy?"

"Come on, Bud," Tristan said, intentionally ignoring Natalie. "We're going cat hunting."

Buddy leaped up, barking.

"Make sure you call me if you find anything," Natalie said. "And wish me luck at the dentist."

"You won't need luck, you'll be fine," Andi said.

"As long as you like fillings and extractions," Tristan added.

Natalie threw a handful of paper clips at him, and laughed.

"Here we are then," said Tristan as he, Andi, and Buddy turned onto Windrush Drive. "I know we really only want to speak with Mr. Channing, but we should look like we're doing regular Pet Finders business. Let's put a poster on this lamppost." He pulled one out of his backpack.

Andi looked along the street. The houses were mostly small, modern, and packed closely together. It seemed odd to think that Tangletree House — which was huge and old — stood on the same road, especially because Andi couldn't see it at all from here. It was set too far back from the sidewalk. "I hope people see the posters," she said. "This street looks very quiet."

They crossed over and hurried up the driveway of the first house.

"Don't talk for too long," Tristan warned as he rang the bell. "It's number nineteen we want."

There was no answer to the doorbell. "Good!" Tristan said. "It'll speed things up if no one's home."

Andi placed a flyer in the mailbox. "You might be wrong about Mr. Channing, you know," she said.

"Wrong? Me? I don't think so." He suddenly looked serious. "We've got to find Lola, Andi. It's really important that we don't let Ms. Giacomo down."

Andi nodded, guessing that he was thinking about Lucy again.

There was nobody home at numbers 3 or 5, but a woman answered the door at number 7. "We're looking for a lost cat," Andi said, handing her a flyer. "Have you seen her?"

"No, sorry." She read the flyer. "But I'll look around in my yard and garage, and I'll call you if I find her."

"Here goes," Tristan said when they reached number 19. They could just see the chimneys of Tangletree House from here. The old house was at the far end of the street, and Andi tried not to look in that direction while they waited for Mr. Channing to open the door. To her relief, Buddy wasn't bothered by being near the house today. He was much more interested in sniffing around Mr. Channing's front porch.

"I bet he can smell Lola," Tristan said. "I told you she — " He broke off as the door opened.

An exceptionally tall man smiled down at them. He was very neat looking. His dark brown hair was slicked back and he wore a gray suit with a pale green shirt and matching tie. "Hello," he said. "What can I do for you?"

He suddenly noticed Buddy and his smile faded. "Keep that dog away," he snapped. "I've got cats in here."

Andi frowned. As if Buddy were likely to hurt his precious cats! She pulled Buddy close to her leg. "Sit, boy," she said. He flopped down at once and she patted him. "He won't go anywhere near your cats," she told Mr. Channing, struggling to keep the irritation out of her voice.

"I'm glad to hear it," Mr. Channing said. "And I'm glad he's well trained. I can't stand people who let their dogs roam around loose. Now, what do you want?"

"We're the Pet Finders Club, and we're looking for a lost cat," Tristan said, holding out one of the flyers. "Have you seen her?"

Mr. Channing took the flyer and scanned it briefly. "Well, this cat looks a lot like my own, but I'm not missing any cats, nor have I seen any lost ones. Sorry."

"She's a Russian Blue," Andi said, nudging Tristan who was craning his neck to see past Mr. Channing. It was obvious he was dying to get inside and poke around, but they couldn't let Mr. Channing know that Tristan suspected him of being a cat-napper. "Her show name's Princess Anastasia," she added.

"Princess Anastasia?" Mr. Channing echoed. He looked at the flyer again. "Of course it is. I recognize her

now. She's Helen Giacomo's cat. Oh, poor Helen! She must be frantic with worry." He looked down at Tristan, who had leaned so far into the hall that his backpack was sweeping against Mr. Channing's legs. "What are you doing?" he demanded.

Tristan turned bright red. "I . . . um . . . I was hoping to see one of your cats. I really love cats and I thought maybe you'd let me come in and visit with them."

"You can't possibly come inside. Not with that dog. I never allow dogs in my house."

"Andi and Buddy could wait outside. . . . " Tristan began.

Before he could finish, there was a meow from inside the house. Buddy leaped forward, barking madly. "Stop it, Buddy!" Andi scolded, hauling on his leash to hold him back. "Bad boy!"

"Listen, I'm sorry but I don't know anything about this missing cat," Mr. Channing said shortly. "So please take your dog away now." He slammed the door shut.

"What an unfriendly man! Imagine not liking dogs!" Andi said as they walked away. "But I still don't think he's taken Lola. He seemed truly upset when he realized it was Ms. Giacomo's cat we were searching for."

"Or he pretended to be."

"Oh, Tristan."

"I think he knows something. For a start, why didn't he recognize Lola right away? I bet he was just pretending not to know her because he's got her locked up."

"I don't know . . . " Andi began.

"And did you see how uncomfortable he looked when I asked if I could come in and see his cats? It was lucky for him Buddy barked when he did. That was a great excuse for keeping me out."

Andi stopped walking and stared at Tristan. "I suppose it does seem a little suspicious."

"A *little*!" Tristan exclaimed. "If you ask me, Mr. Channing knows exactly what's happened to Lola!"

Chapter Four

It was nearly six o'clock when Andi said good-bye to Tristan.

"I'd better go see my parents," he said, "in case they've forgotten what I look like. See you tomorrow."

"Time for a run, Bud," Andi said when Tristan had gone. If Coach Wallace was going to choose her to play in the next soccer game, she needed to shape up.

She began to jog along the sidewalk with Buddy scampering beside her. She took a longer route home than normal, but she managed to find her way easily. Although she'd only lived in Orchard Park for a couple of months, she hardly ever got lost now like she had when she and her mom had first moved here.

"Almost home now, Bud," she said, spotting a mailbox painted with turquoise peacock feathers. The mailbox belonged to Mr. Wheeler, who lived on the next street over from hers.

Suddenly, Buddy jerked away. His leash slipped through Andi's fingers and he charged into Mr. Wheeler's front yard.

"Buddy!" Andi yelled. "Come here!"

As he bounded across the lawn, trailing his leash, a small, whitish dog sprang out of some bushes and dashed up to him. Andi recognized the dog at once. It was the one she and Natalie had seen at the park.

The two dogs barked playfully, then darted around the side of the house. "Buddy, no!" Andi cried, hurtling after them.

Mr. Wheeler was sitting in his backyard, with his back to Andi, dabbing paint on a canvas that was balanced on an artist's easel. He was wearing a bulky coat and a blue wool hat that almost entirely hid his thick white hair.

"Mr. Wheeler!" Andi called. "Look out!"

The old man glanced around just as the dogs reached him. Buddy dove under the easel, making it rock on its spindly wooden legs. Several tubes of paint, a palette knife, two paintbrushes, and a fresh painter's cloth tumbled onto the grass. The smaller dog circled Mr. Wheeler, barking loudly, then shot forward, seized the cloth in her mouth, and darted away with it.

Mr. Wheeler grabbed the easel to steady it.

"I'm so sorry, Mr. Wheeler," Andi panted, running after Buddy. "Buddy saw that other dog in your front yard and he got away from me." The dogs were playing a tug-of-war game with the cloth in the middle of the lawn. "Stop it, Buddy!" Andi scolded. Darting toward him, she managed to grab the end of his leash. "Bad Buddy! Bad boy!"

Buddy's tail and ears drooped. He slunk toward her, aware that he'd misbehaved, and pressed himself against her legs.

"What are we going to do about the other one?" Mr. Wheeler asked. The oatmeal-colored dog was rummaging around in a row of bushes near the street. "I don't want to risk picking her up, in case she gets scared. Most dogs are perfectly safe, but you never know."

"I've got some of Buddy's dog treats in my pocket," Andi said. "You might be able to catch her with those." She handed the bag to Mr. Wheeler.

He tossed one onto the lawn a few feet in front of the strange dog. She trotted over to it, her tail wagging. She wolfed down the treat then looked hopefully at Mr. Wheeler with her head to one side.

"She looks as though she's got a little Border terrier in her," Andi said, admiring her cute, boxy head and pricked up ears.

"I think you're right," Mr. Wheeler agreed. He threw another dog treat. "Here, girl!"

The dog ran to it and gobbled it down. "She likes these," Mr. Wheeler said as the little dog jumped up and planted her paws on his knee.

The old man let her sniff his hand, then he reached down to pet her. She squirmed with pleasure, her tail wagging hard. "What a friendly little thing!" he said. "I wonder who she belongs to."

"I think she's lost," Andi said. She told Mr. Wheeler about seeing the dog in the park.

"So, what will you do with her now?" he asked.

"I could take her home with me while we try to find her owner," Andi suggested.

"You come along with me then, young lady," said Mr. Wheeler, patting the lost dog, "and I'll find you a temporary leash." He went indoors with the dog trotting at his heels. A moment later, they reappeared with a piece of thick cord twisted through the dog's collar. "This should last until you get her home."

"Thanks." Andi retrieved the cloth that the dogs had been playing with and picked up the paintbrushes. "What a great picture!" she said. Mr. Wheeler was painting the trees at the end of his yard in their fall colors.

"Thanks. The trees are so beautiful this year that I just had to get out here and paint." Mr. Wheeler handed her the makeshift leash, then sat down at his easel again. "I think I've got time for a few more leaves before the light goes."

"I'll see you." Andi led the two dogs around the side of the house and headed for home. They trotted beside her, nuzzling each other, their tails wagging furiously. "Anyone would think you two had known each other for years!" Andi laughed. "I guess you like making friends as much as I do, Bud!"

Mrs. Talbot was in the kitchen when Andi came in with the two dogs. "Who's this?" she asked, looking down at the visitor in surprise.

"I'm going to call her Oat," Andi said, "because of her color. She's lost, and we need to find her owner."

"You'd better take her to the ASPCA," said Mrs. Talbot. She glanced at the clock on the wall. "But it's closed now, so she'll have to stay with us tonight." She laughed. "I don't know! You guys started out as the Pet Finders Club, but now you seem to be going into the pet hotel business, as well!"

Andi grinned. That sounded pretty cool to her.

* * *

Natalie and Tristan arrived at Andi's house just before nine o'clock the next morning. Andi had called to tell them about Oat the evening before.

"What a sweetie!" Natalie said, as Oat squirmed around her legs, her tail wagging.

"She seems pretty healthy," Tristan said, as the little dog jumped up at him, "so she probably hasn't been lost for long."

"What should we do with her?" Natalie asked.

"Mom thinks we should take her to the ASPCA," Andi said. "They're open on Saturday mornings."

"They've got a microchip scanner, too," Tristan added. "So if Oat's been chipped, we'll find out who her owner is right away — like we did with Jet, remember?"

They may have gotten lucky with microchips once before, but Andi didn't want to get her hopes up too high this time around. She tried to think about other things while her mom drove them to the ASPCA center, but even then, all she could think about were bad thoughts: Agnes Delaney's ghost, Lola's disappearance. . . . Nothing could distract her from gloomy thoughts.

"I'll wait in the car," Mrs. Talbot offered when they'd arrived. "I'm not sure there'd be room for all of us in there."

The Pet Finders hurried inside the ASPCA building

with Oat. Fisher Pearce, the resident veterinarian and a friend of Christine Wilson, came out to greet them. "Hey, you guys! Caught any thieves recently?" he joked as he showed them into his consulting room. "Who's this?"

"We call her Oat," Andi told him. "She's lost. We thought she might be microchipped."

"Let's hope she is." Fisher lifted Oat onto the table and ran a handheld scanner over the fur on her neck. "No luck, I'm afraid," he said, when the green light didn't flash. "And we've had no reports of lost dogs lately. Looks like it's the kennel for you, girl." He rubbed Oat's chest and she licked his hand.

"I can keep her for now while we try to track down her owner," Andi suggested. Oat was so cute, she didn't want to think of her being in an unfamiliar kennel.

Fisher looked thoughtful. "Have you asked your mom about this?"

"Not yet. But I'm sure she won't mind. She's outside in the car now. I could run out and ask her."

"Okay," Fisher agreed. "You do that, while I give Oat a quick health check."

Andi raced outside. "Mom, you've got to let me keep Oat while we try to find her owner, okay? Please? She's not microchipped, so she'll have to stay in the kennel if you don't let her stay with us."

Mrs. Talbot sighed. "I don't see why not. She's adorable, and she and Buddy are the best of friends already."

"Oh, thank you!" Andi hugged her mom, then ran back inside. "She said yes!" she announced, bursting into the consulting room.

Fisher lifted Oat down from the table. "That's great," he said. "Now let me find a leash to lend you. You'll never be able to take her for walks on this cord." He opened a cupboard and began to rummage through the shelves. "What other cases are you Pet Finders working on at the moment?"

"We're looking for a missing Russian Blue cat," Natalie told him.

Fisher looked around in surprise. "A Russian Blue? That's funny. I was at Paul Channing's house this morning, delivering some Russian Blue kittens. His regular vet, Dr. Harvey, is on vacation. Poor man, he's probably the most anxious pet owner I've ever met! Phoned me three times on Thursday to tell me how his cat was doing, and four times yesterday." He dove into the cupboard again. "Still, it all ended happily. The kittens are beautiful."

Tristan nudged Andi in the ribs. "See?" he hissed. "Those kittens have got to be Lola's!"

Chapter Five

"Let's walk home," Natalie suggested. "Your mom won't mind going back without us, will she, Andi?"

"I don't think so." Andi left Natalie holding Oat on her new leash and ran to the car. "Is it okay if we walk back, Mom?"

"Sure. It'll give me a chance to pick up some groceries. I'll see you at home later." Mrs. Talbot drove away.

"I guess that proves it," Tristan said, as Andi joined him and Natalie again. "Mr. Channing's got a cat with kittens. He *has* to be the thief."

Andi wasn't so sure. "Maybe it's just a coincidence. Both cats might have been expecting kittens at the same time."

"No way," Tristan argued. "Lola is at Mr. Channing's — and we've got to find a way to get in there."

"What about Oat?" Andi asked to change the subject. She had a bad feeling that Tristan might march over to Mr. Channing's house right now and barge inside.

Oat gave a bark as if to say she wished they'd hurry up and get her home.

"We could make posters with DO YOU KNOW THIS DOG? at the top, and a picture of Oat underneath," Natalie suggested.

"Good idea!" Tristan agreed. "It's lucky — " He broke off suddenly. "Hey, there's a store over there. I need a snack."

"You can't be hungry!" Andi exclaimed. "Didn't you have any breakfast?"

"Breakfast was ages ago." He darted across the road and into the store. He came out a moment later with a granola bar and a copy of the local newspaper.

"I just realized something. Papers have a classified ad section."

"And your point is?"

"I know what Tris means," said Andi. "Somebody might be advertising about it if they've lost Oat!" She took the paper and flicked through it until she found the right page. "Here!"

They all crowded around to see. There were ads selling goldfish and baby hamsters, but nobody had lost a dog. Then Tristan suddenly stabbed the page with an accusing finger. "There! Look! Russian Blue kittens for sale. And the phone number has an Orchard Park area code. It must be Mr. Channing."

"They can't be Lola's," Natalie said. "Mr. Channing can't be clueless enough to advertise a stolen cat's kittens."

"Someone would find out, and he'd be arrested," Andi added.

"But now we'll have an excuse to go into his house. We can pretend that one of us wants to buy a kitten. That way we'll get to see the mother," Tristan said, exasperated. "Don't you care about finding Lola? Ms. Giacomo's going out of her mind with worry, and you two just keep insisting that Mr. Channing hasn't got her."

"Of course we care," Andi said. "But there's no proof that Mr. Channing's taken her. We have to think of other possibilities, too, Tristan."

"Such as?"

Andi and Natalie looked at each other. The posters hadn't inspired any calls yet, and their search hadn't turned up any clues. "Okay," Andi sighed. "There's no harm in looking at the kittens' mother, I guess. And if she does turn out to be Lola, then that will be another case solved."

Natalie took out her cell phone. "I'll call now and make an appointment." She punched in the number.

They waited impatiently for someone to answer, then Natalie gave them a thumbs-up. "Hello," she said. "I saw your ad for kittens, and I'd like to come and see them. My parents are thinking of buying me a kitten for my birthday."

There was a pause while Natalie listened.

"She sounds gorgeous," she said. "What's the address? Okay, I'll see you later, then. Thanks!" She switched off her phone. "It's Mr. Channing's ad, all right. That was his wife. She says the mother cat is called Snowdrop of the Steppes."

"More like Lola!" Tristan snorted.

"I'm going over there this afternoon at one thirty," Natalie continued.

"Great," Andi said.

"One thirty?" Tristan echoed.

"What's wrong with that?"

"I'm helping out at Paws for Thought. Can't you change the appointment for later? I'll be done by four o'clock."

"Sorry, that was the only time Mr. and Mrs. Channing were free," Natalie said.

"You'll be able to ask Christine's customers about

Oat, Tristan," Andi pointed out. "Maybe one of them will know someone who's lost a dog."

Tristan shrugged. "I guess." He bent down to stroke the little dog's head. "Don't you worry, girl. We'll find out where you're from soon."

Andi and Natalie met outside Mr. Channing's house just before one thirty. Natalie was dressed in a pair of faded jeans and a beaded pink top that Andi had seen in the window of a boutique on Main Street. "You look great," she said.

"I thought I'd better look like my parents have plenty of money. Russian Blue kittens are probably expensive. Do you like this top?"

"Love it." Andi fingered the row of beads that ran around the edge of the sleeve. "But the jeans look a little old."

"Old! I just bought them last week. They're the latest style!"

"Sorry," Andi laughed. "Come on, we'd better go in." She glanced down the road toward the chimneys of Tangletree House and shivered.

Mr. Channing opened the front door to them. "Hello," he said. He looked at Andi in surprise. "Aren't you the girl who came here looking for Princess Anastasia?"

Andi froze, then thought fast. "Oh, yeah! That's right. Isn't it funny that my friend wants to buy one of your kittens?"

"Uh, yes, but I hope you haven't brought your dog with you."

"No, he's at home."

Andi and Natalie followed Mr. Channing inside. They crossed a cluttered hallway, dodging a shopping basket, two sports bags, and a pair of battered jogging shoes. Then Mr. Channing ushered them into a cozy living room with a fire crackling in the hearth. A cat lay in a basket beside the fire with four tiny gray kittens curled up next to her. Two were the same silver-gray as their mother, one was a little darker with silver-tipped ears, and the fourth was the color of the sky on a rainy day.

"Oh, they're so cute!" Natalie exclaimed, as if she'd forgotten she was only pretending to be interested. She knelt beside the basket and picked up the darkest kitten. It gave a tiny purr, then snuggled down in her hands.

"You do realize that they won't be able to leave their mother for another eight weeks?" Mr. Channing said.

"Yes. But that will be okay," Natalie replied. "I don't mind waiting."

"I'll leave you to get to know them," Mr. Channing

said. "I'll be in the kitchen if you need me. The mother's name is Snowdrop." He went out.

Andi took out the photo of Lola. Mr. Channing's cat was much paler, but her face was disturbingly similar, with the same wide, green eyes and friendly expression. "I don't think this is Lola," she said, peering closely at the cat in the basket.

Natalie didn't reply. She was holding the kitten next to her face and stroking it with one finger.

"Nat!" Andi shoved the photo under Natalie's nose. "What do you think? Is this cat Lola?"

"Oh, sorry. This kitten is so sweet!"

"We came to look at the mother," Andi reminded her.

Natalie frowned at the photo, then looked at the cat. "Her fur's paler than Lola's."

"That's what I thought," Andi said. "Tristan was *way* wrong about this."

"Unless Mr. Channing's dyed her."

"Dyed her? Can you dye cats?"

"I don't see why not. People have their hair dyed all the time. What's the difference?"

Andi admitted that Nat had a point. She bent over the basket and rubbed the cat's fur, flattening it down until she could see right to the end of some of the hairs. If she'd been dyed, there'd be a trace of darker fur

close to her skin where the hairs were growing out. The cat began to purr and pressed her head against Andi's sleeve.

"Can you see anything?" Natalie asked.

"Her fur's pale all the way through. She's definitely not Lola. We were right all along. Mr. Channing doesn't have anything to do with Lola's disappearance." She picked up the smallest kitten and held it against her chest. The tiny creature felt like it was made of feathers. "I wish you were really buying one, Nat," Andi whispered. "They're adorable."

"Me, too."

Andi began to feel uncomfortably hot being so close to the fire. "I'm boiling," she complained. "I'm just going to ask Mr. Channing for a glass of water, then we should leave."

"What are we going to say about the kittens?"

"Say you'll think it over." Andi carefully put the kitten back in the basket and watched, enchanted, as it snuggled against its mother's side again. "I won't be long." She went out into the hall, shutting the living room door behind her so the kittens couldn't get out.

At the end of the hall, the door was ajar and Andi could hear Mr. and Mrs. Channing talking in the kitchen.

"I don't know what to do," Mr. Channing was saying.

"Well, I think you should tell that girl what you saw," his wife replied.

Andi gasped. Was Mrs. Channing talking about her? She crept closer, feeling like a spy.

"How can I?" Mr. Channing demanded. "I've already told her and her friend that I don't know anything."

Andi's heart began to pound. Mr. Channing had been lying all along. He *did* know something about Lola's disappearance!

Chapter Six

"I'm going to go see how the girls are getting along with the kittens," Mr. Channing said, his voice getting louder as if he was moving toward the door.

Andi darted back along the hall and burst into the living room.

Natalie looked up in astonishment. "What's happened?"

"I can't tell you now." Andi quickly shut the door. Then she flung herself down beside the basket of kittens and began to stroke the one nearest to her.

Mr. Channing came in. "Have you decided which one you'd like?"

"Not yet," Natalie sighed, picking up a different kitten. "I think I need a little longer. They're all so gorgeous."

Andi flashed her a horrified look. "We've got to go," she mouthed, keeping her back toward Mr. Channing.

"Actually," Natalie said hastily, catching Andi's look, "I should talk to my parents about which one to get, too." She put the kitten she was holding back into the basket and stood up.

"Don't take too long to decide, or I may have sold them all," warned Mr. Channing. "Russian Blues are very popular."

"I won't." Natalie looked back wistfully at the kittens as Mr. Channing showed them out into the hall. Another Russian Blue cat was coming down the stairs. Andi stared at it, wondering if it could be Lola. "You've got two cats," she said.

"That's right. This is Beauty."

Andi clicked her fingers and the cat ran to her. She petted it, but she could see, now that it was close to her, that it couldn't possibly be Lola. It was much too big. Ms. Giacomo had said Lola was a small cat.

"What was all that about?" Natalie demanded when the front door closed behind them.

"Wait until we're away from the house," Andi whispered dramatically.

As they came out of the front yard, they saw Tristan flying down the sidewalk toward them. "How did it go?" he called. He jumped off his skateboard and snatched it up before the wheels stopped spinning.

"What are you doing here?" said Andi. "I thought you were helping out at Paws for Thought."

"I was, but Christine let me go early. Did you find Lola?"

"No, but Mr. Channing definitely knows something." Andi told them what she'd overheard as they walked away from the house.

"It doesn't sound as though he's cat-napped Lola himself," Natalie said thoughtfully. "But he obviously saw something important."

"I bet he knows exactly where Lola is," Tristan insisted. "We should go back right now and ask him to tell us everything."

"He'd only lie," Natalie pointed out. "He'd probably say Andi misheard and that he wasn't talking about Lola at all."

"Or he'd yell at us for spying on him," Andi added.

"But we've got to do something!" Tristan argued. "Ms. Giacomo is relying on us to find Lola."

"I know," Andi said. "I'm worried about Lola, too. But there's no point in asking Mr. Channing. We'll have to think of another way to find out what he saw."

"Come back to my place so we can talk about it," Tristan said.

It was nearly two thirty when they arrived at Tristan's

house. Dean, Tristan's fifteen-year-old brother, was coming down the stairs, listening to his headphones. "Hey," he said, pushing the headphones down around his neck. "What's up?"

Tristan told him what Andi had overheard at Mr. Channing's house. "We think he must have seen Lola someplace."

"Sounds like it," Dean agreed. "What are you gonna do about it?"

"We were kind of hoping to come up with some more ideas about that," Andi admitted.

"We've searched everywhere we can think of," Tristan added gloomily. "We've been down every street, looked under every parked car. . . . "

Dean sat down on the stairs, frowning thoughtfully. "So you don't think Lola's hiding near Mr. Channing's house?"

"No."

"He might have seen her somewhere else, then. Maybe she wandered farther than you thought. Maybe he spotted her on his way home from somewhere."

"Of course!" Natalie burst out. "We just need to figure out where he goes regularly. Then we can follow his route and look for possible hiding places. That's a great idea, Dean!"

Dean grinned at her from under a wisp of his spiky blond hair. Natalie turned bright red and fiddled with her friendship bracelet.

"I think it's a dumb idea," Tristan said. "We don't know where Mr. Channing works or shops or anything."

"We might be able to find out, though," Andi pointed out.

Dean agreed. "You should consider yourself lucky, Tris, to have a brother with good looks *and* brains." Laughing, he went along the hall and out into the backyard.

"Good looks!" Tristan hooted. "Brains! He must be joking."

Andi grinned. "I know someone who thinks he's good-looking." She looked pointedly at Nat.

"You have a crush on my brother?" Tristan said, staring at Natalie. "Are you crazy?"

Natalie glared at him. "It's none of your business who I like, Tristan! And if — "

"So how are we going to find out where Mr. Channing works and stuff?" Andi interrupted before they started another round of bickering.

"We can't follow him from his house if he drives his car most of the time," Tristan pointed out. "Not even *you* could run fast enough to keep up with a car, Andi."

"Fisher might know where he works," Natalie said. "He probably has all of Mr. Channing's contact information after helping with Snowdrop's kittens."

"That's right!" Tristan noted, seemingly having forgiven Natalie for liking his brother. Then his face fell. "But how can we ask him? He'll want to know why we need the information. He might think we're plotting, like when we found our last thief's hideaway."

They moved into the kitchen. Andi and Natalie sat on stools at the breakfast bar while Tristan poured orange juice into three glasses. They sipped their drinks in silence, thinking hard.

At last, Andi spoke up. "What about Oat? We can't forget her. Did you have any luck with finding her owner, Tristan?"

"No." He set down his glass. "I bet if nobody knows anything about her, she probably came from out of town. Maybe she just walked here."

"I don't think so." Andi shook her head. "Her paws weren't sore, and she looked well-fed."

"Yeah, but she might have stopped at diners, like Buddy did," Natalie reminded her.

"Maybe she belongs to someone who was visiting Orchard Park?" Tristan suggested.

"I hope not," Andi said. "If she does, then putting up posters won't help because her owner won't be around to see them."

"Then we'll need to find a new way of tracking lost owners," Natalie said. "But we haven't even made the posters yet. Let's go over to your house now and get to work on them."

After school on Monday afternoon, the Pet Finders met to walk their dogs. Andi had brought Buddy and Oat, Natalie had Jet, and Tristan had borrowed Christine's cocker spaniel, Max.

The four dogs rushed up to one another, barking excitedly.

"Whoa, Jet!" Natalie shrieked as the excited black Lab almost pulled her down. She regained her balance. "Sometimes I wonder why I like dogs!"

"Because they're cute and cuddly," Andi said, giving Buddy an affectionate pat.

As they headed for the park, they passed one of the posters they'd made for Oat. They had stuck twenty of them to lampposts on the roads surrounding the park the day before. "That's you, Oat!" Andi said, stopping to look at it. She sighed. "I wish somebody would call and claim you."

Just then, a truck came rumbling along the road. At once, Oat pulled toward it, whining.

"What's she doing?" Andi asked, puzzled. They stopped to watch as Oat strained toward the truck. But when it sped by, she sank down dejectedly on the sidewalk.

"What's wrong with her?" said Natalie.

Andi crouched beside her. "I don't know." She stroked Oat's head, but the little dog didn't even look at her. "Come on, Oat," Andi coaxed. "Cheer up, girl." She looked anxiously at Natalie and Tristan. "I haven't seen her like this before. Do you think she's sick?"

Buddy trotted over. He licked Oat's face, then nudged her with his nose as though he were trying to make her stand up.

Oat turned her head away with a mournful sigh.

A second truck appeared. At once, the little dog leaped up again. She began to bark eagerly, her strange mood forgotten. But once the truck had passed them, she just slumped down again.

"It's the trucks that are making her act like this," Andi said. "Do you think she's frightened of the noise they make?"

"Maybe," Tristan said. "Come on, though. Let's not hang around if they're upsetting her."

They pulled Oat to her feet and walked on. Several cars sped by, but Oat didn't notice them at all.

"Not all the traffic's bothering her," Natalie remarked. "She's not even *looking* at the cars."

A furniture truck approached. As expected now, Oat halted, quivering with excitement, then strained toward the truck, pulling so hard against her leash that Andi's fingers went numb. Tristan grabbed the leash, too. "It's all right, girl," he said. "It's only a truck."

"You know what?" said Natalie, looking down at Oat. "She's not scared at all. It's like she's really *happy* to see the trucks."

The third truck rumbled past, and Oat sank down again as if she'd lost her favorite toy and a juicy bone all at once.

Andi got an idea then. "Maybe she came to Orchard Park in a truck?" she suggested. "Could she have been trapped in a moving van or delivery truck without anyone noticing? I've heard of cats doing that."

Tristan shook his head. "Wouldn't she be afraid of trucks if that had happened? She'd think they were going to take her away again. No, I think she's used to riding in trucks because . . . because . . . " He trailed off.

"Because her owner's a truck driver!" Natalie finished triumphantly, holding up her hand for a high five.

"So maybe she was left behind when he made a delivery to a store or something!" Andi said.

"But there are tons of stores in Orchard Park," Tristan pointed out. "We can't go to every one to ask if anyone recognizes her. It'll take years."

"Why don't we go back to where we first saw her in the park?" suggested Natalie. "That might lead to some clues."

Tristan took Buddy's leash, and Andi picked Oat up. The little dog was too miserable to even walk. Andi hugged her tight, trying to make her feel better. "We'll find your owner soon, Oat," she promised.

As soon as they reached the park, Tristan let Buddy and Max off their leashes. They raced away, then circled back and barked at Oat. She lifted her head from Andi's shoulder and squirmed to be put down. "Don't let her off her leash," Natalie warned. "We don't want her running off again."

"Come on," Andi said. "Let's run." Holding tight to Oat's leash, she sprinted across the grass with Oat running beside her, and Buddy and Max hard on her heels. She headed in the direction of the woods, then veered off to the right, trying to remember exactly where she and Natalie had been when they'd first spotted Oat. She reached a clump of bushes and stopped to look back. Tristan and Natalie were a long way behind. "Hurry up!" she yelled.

They reached her at last, panting hard. "It's all right for you," Tristan puffed. "You're a soccer player and a track star, but some of us have less energetic hobbies."

Andi laughed. "You should come jogging with me, Tristan. And you, too, Natalie."

"No, thanks," Natalie said firmly. "I think I'll stick to chess."

"Is this the place where you first saw Oat?" Tristan asked.

"I think so," Andi said.

"No, it was farther over," Natalie said. "Past that tree there."

Andi looked where she was pointing. "No, it wasn't. We came around the pond and headed for the woods." She caught sight of a cluster of thorny, leafless bushes with a few shriveled roses attached. "There!" she said. "Those rosebushes. We walked right past them. I remember catching my coat on a thorn."

"Yeah, but we crossed a path, too," Natalie said. "And there's no path near the roses so . . . "

"Oat, no!" Andi yelled.

Oat had jerked free while they were busy arguing. She raced away, trailing her leash behind her.

"Come back!" Tristan shouted.

They sped after her. Andi soon left Tristan and Natalie a long way behind, but the distance between her and Oat was growing wider by the second. She was afraid she wouldn't catch up, and that the little dog would be lost again.

Buddy darted along beside Andi, his little legs pumping furiously. Andi pushed herself harder than ever, but Oat just seemed to move even quicker. Suddenly, to Andi's relief, Oat reached a path and stopped. She began to sniff along the ground as though she was trying to figure out the right way to go.

"Oat!" Andi panted, slowing a little. "Here, girl."

The little dog looked up and wagged her tail.

Andi stopped running. She approached Oat cautiously, worried that she might take off again.

Oat went on sniffing, occasionally lifting her head to sneak a glance at Andi. As soon as she was close enough, Andi grabbed her leash. "Don't you run off again," she scolded, ruffling Oat's ears. She looked around and saw Natalie and Tristan sauntering toward her. "Take your time!" she called sarcastically.

"We didn't want to spoil your fun," Tristan said. "You're always saying you need to work out more, and that seemed like a perfect opportunity."

"We didn't want to pass you and embarrass you," Natalie added, nudging Tristan.

"We were trying to figure out where we were when we first saw Oat," Andi reminded them sternly. "And I still think we were somewhere near those rosebushes."

Natalie opened her mouth to argue but before she could speak, Tristan cut in. "Don't start arguing again. It doesn't matter where *you* were standing when you saw Oat. What matters is where *she* was."

Andi nodded. "I guess you're right."

"Don't tell him that," Natalie groaned. "He'll go on about it for days."

Andi looked around. "This is where we saw her," she said. "She was running along this path. Then she disappeared into that patch of shrubbery. Clever girl, Oat! She must have known what we were saying. Where does the path go, Tristan? Are there any stores near here where a truck would make deliveries?"

"No, this path just leads to the road out of town."

Natalie sighed. "I really thought we were onto something there."

"Wait. We still might be!" Andi turned to Tristan.

"Where do trucks stop in Orchard Park? You know, when the drivers need food and stuff."

He frowned. "There are a few places. There's a café at the rest stop on Half Mile Lane, and one on Belvedere Road. Oh, and there's an overnight truck park on Stratton Street."

"Which one's closest to here?"

"Half Mile Lane." Tristan smiled. "And this path runs really close to it. You might be onto something, Andi."

"Careful," Natalie warned. "We don't want Andi getting a swelled head, too."

Andi laughed. "You're just jealous because you didn't think of it yourself."

"Come on!" Tristan whooped. "What are we waiting for?"

Andi shot away at first, then slowed to a jog to allow the others to catch up with her. It wouldn't be fair if she found Oat's owner by herself, but she was impatient to reach the truck stop. It would be fantastic to see Oat reunited with her owner.

The café at the rest stop was a one-story concrete building set in the middle of a huge parking lot. Trucks of all sizes, from enormous semis with double trailers to small delivery vans, were parked all around the lot.

"This place is certainly popular," Andi said. "I wonder if Oat's owner is here right now."

A burly man came out of the café then, wiping his fingers on a paper towel. He glanced at them, then stopped and stared. "Apple?" he exclaimed. "Apple? Is that you?"

Oat gave a bark of recognition and lurched forward. Her leash slipped through Andi's fingers yet again as she hustled across the cement toward the man.

Tristan grinned triumphantly and gave Andi a high five. "Looks like the Pet Finders have just closed another case!"

Chapter Seven

"Where did you find her?" the man called, as Oat leaped around him.

"In the park a couple of days ago," Andi replied. "She's been staying with me while we tried to track you down. We're the Pet Finders Club." She beamed at the man. "I guess we can stop looking now."

"Oh, no," the man said. "Apple's not *my* dog. She belongs to Pete, one of the Sun-Ripe drivers." He bent down to pick up the end of Apple's leash, and she jumped up to lick his cheek. "You rascal," he laughed, rubbing her head.

"Not yours!" Natalie said with disbelief. "I don't suppose Pete's here now, is he?"

The man glanced around the truck park. "I don't see his rig. And I don't know how to get in touch with him, either, I'm afraid. We just share a table sometimes when we meet up here." He handed the leash to Andi. "I'd love to help you find him, but I've got to go. Otherwise, I'll have my boss breathing down my neck."

"Uh, okay. Thanks for telling us about Pete," said Tristan.

"Did he say Pete drove for Sun-Ripe?" Natalie asked as his truck drove away.

"That's right," Andi replied.

Natalie pointed to the main road that ran past the truck stop. "There's a Sun-Ripe truck now."

They raced across the parking lot toward the truck waving and yelling, but the driver roared past them without stopping. "There's a phone number on the side!" Andi yelled. "Quick, does anyone have a pen?"

"Don't worry about it, I got it!" Tristan said, as the truck disappeared around the corner. "My head is bursting with information, and the Sun-Ripe phone number and address are in there now, too."

"I don't believe you," Natalie said. "I know you think you're some sort of Memory Man, but nobody can remember a phone number they saw that quickly. And the address was written in really tiny letters."

Tristan shrugged and then recited the number and the address right off the top of his head.

"You're amazing," Andi said in awe.

* * *

They hurried back to Andi's house to phone Sun-Ripe. "Remember that number, Tristan," she urged, as they raced across her lawn to the front door. Andi couldn't help getting her hopes up this time. All the information they'd stumbled on in the last hour was simply too much to let them down.

"I won't forget it," promised Tristan. "I think I know my own brain better than you do."

They crowded through the Talbots' front door and into the hallway, where Andi grabbed the phone. "Okay, what was it?" she asked hurriedly.

Tristan recited the number while Andi dialed, though he paused a few times to pretend he'd lost it. When she'd finally dialed the entire number, it only took a moment before her call was answered. "Sun-Ripe. How may I help you?"

"Hello," Andi said. "I've found a dog named Apple, and I think it belongs to one of your drivers. His name's Pete."

"Oh, how wonderful!" the receptionist cried. "Pete will be so relieved! He's been terribly worried about Apple. Is she all right?"

"She's fine," Andi said.

"That's such good news! Give me your address, and I'll call Pete on his cell phone to tell him the dog's safe."

Andi gave her address.

"Pete's only about twenty minutes from there now," the lady said. "I'll tell him to come right over."

Andi beamed at Tristan and Natalie as she hung up the receiver. "He's on his way," she said. "Do you hear that, Oat — I mean Apple? Your owner's coming for you!"

Apple rolled over so that Andi could stroke her tummy, then she leaped up, raced up the stairs and down again, and finally shot into the living room with the other dogs tearing behind her.

"Let's go and tell my mom the good news," Andi said, heading for the kitchen.

Pete was a huge grizzly-bear of a man, with a bushy beard and a crinkly-eyed smile. The moment Andi opened the door to him, Apple leaped into his arms, and he hugged her tightly. The little dog almost disappeared in his giant hands. "Apple! Where have you been? I thought you'd gone for good, girl."

"Come on in," Andi said, feeling a bit shy.

Pete followed her into the living room where Natalie and Tristan were waiting. Buddy, Jet, and Max were dozing on the sofa in a tangle of furry legs and tails.

"Thank you so much for finding her for me," Pete

said. He sat down and Apple squirmed onto his lap, licking his face, his hands, his ears. . . .

"It's what we do," Tristan explained. "We're the Pet Finders Club."

"Really? So you find lost pets and then locate their owners?"

"Yes. And owners call us if they've lost a pet, too, so we can track it down."

"What a great idea!" Pete said. "It's lucky Apple chose to jump out of my truck in Orchard Park, of all places. We might not have been so lucky if you three hadn't found her."

"How did she get lost?" Andi asked.

"She was asleep in my cab when I stopped at Half Mile Lane. There's a ledge behind the driver's seat and she curls up there sometimes for a nap." He broke off, laughing, as Apple licked his nose. "It was a sunny day," he continued, "and it was hot in my cab, so I left the window open when I went into the café to get a coffee. When I came out, I didn't think to check on Apple. I just assumed she'd still be on her ledge, asleep."

"So she jumped out while you were in the café?" Natalie asked.

"Must have. When I got to my next stop, she wasn't there. I was horrified, I can tell you. But I couldn't turn back. You can't be late with fruit. It doesn't keep. You have to stick to your schedule." He hugged Apple again. "I've had a terrible few days, wondering where this little lady had gone to." He smiled at the Pet Finders. "You kids are great! If it hadn't been for you . . . " He took out a large handkerchief and blew his nose. "Well, I might never have seen Apple again."

"We're glad you're back together again," Tristan said, looking rather uncomfortable at Pete's display of emotion.

Pete put Apple down and stood up. "We'd better hit the road. I'm due back at the depot."

The Pet Finders petted Apple one last time. "No more jumping out of windows," Andi warned.

"No chance of that," said Pete. "From now on, I'm keeping her right with me." He shook hands with them all. "Thanks again for everything."

He opened the truck door and helped tiny Apple jump in. She darted across to the passenger seat and stood with her front paws on the dash, her tongue lolling and her tail wagging furiously.

Pete climbed in after her, started the engine, and honked the horn at the kids. "Thanks!" he called out the window as he drove away.

"I'm going to miss Apple," Andi sighed. "It was kind of fun having two dogs, as well as a new best friend for Buddy to play with."

"I'll miss her, too," agreed Natalie.

"Buddy will be sorry she's gone," Andi added.

"Yeah, but he'll get his basket all to himself again," Tristan pointed out. "And we've solved another case. I think this calls for a celebration smoothie. Anyone up for the Banana Beach Café? You never know, we might see Fisher. Maybe we'll come up with some way of finding out where Mr. Channing works."

The Banana Beach Café was one of Andi's favorite places in Orchard Park. The building was painted brilliant yellow, and the tables outside had rainbow-colored sun umbrellas that brightened up the place even when the sky was gray. It was run by Maggie and Jango Pearce, Fisher's mom and dad.

Andi and Tristan left Natalie sitting outside on a bench with the dogs while they went inside to order. "Say hello to Long John for me," she called after them.

Long John Silver, a beautiful green-and-blue parrot, was strutting along the counter. "Bananas!" he squawked as they walked in.

"Hello, Long John," Andi said, stroking the parrot's feathery chest.

The parrot rubbed his head against her hand. "Bananas!" he repeated. "More bananas!"

"Hey, Tristan! Hello, Andi!" Maggie Pearce cried, hurrying out of the back room so that the beaded curtain covering the doorway rattled madly. "Jango! Look who it is!" She was a beaming, round-faced Jamaican woman, and today, as usual, she wore a dress the color of sunflowers. She was carrying a milk jug that she set down on the counter.

"Hi, Maggie," said Tristan.

"Hello, Mrs. Pearce," Andi said, smiling.

Jango Pearce, a plump man with tufts of gray hair at his temples, came out to greet them. He was wearing an apron decorated with palm trees and a baseball cap with a huge sunflower sprouting from the top. "What do you think of my new hat?" he asked, turning around to give them a side view.

"It's certainly bright, Mr. Pearce," Andi said carefully.

"That's good! There's no place in Seattle as sunny as the Banana Beach."

Long John Silver sidled over to the milk jug and tried to dip his beak into it.

"No, you don't," Maggie scolded, tapping his head.

The parrot hopped away. "Bananas," he grumbled. "More bananas." He gave a sudden shriek that made everyone jump.

"Just listen to that bird!" Jango chuckled. "He sure knows how to get attention."

"What can I get you?" asked Maggie.

"Three banana-spice smoothies, please," Tristan said.

"Three?"

"Natalie's outside with the dogs," he explained.

"You go sit down, and I'll bring them right out," Maggie said, as Jango disappeared through the beaded curtain to make the smoothies.

Andi and Tristan went outside and sat down. "We must be crazy, sitting outside in November," Andi said, shivering.

"You shouldn't be cold," Natalie said. "You're wearing about twenty layers of clothes."

"Only a sweater, a fleece, and a padded jacket," Andi protested. "What I really need is a couple of blankets and a huge wool hat to cover my ears."

"You'll get used to the weather here, eventually," Tristan said. "And then you'll wonder what you ever saw in all that Florida sunshine."

Maggie soon came out carrying a tray of smoothies. There was a rainbow-colored straw and a yellow paper umbrella in each glass. "Here you go," she said, setting the tray down on the table. "And how are you, Natalie?" she asked.

"I'm fine, thanks, Mrs. Pearce."

Maggie stooped down to stroke the dogs. "You still finding those missing pets?" she asked.

Before they could reply, a deep voice made them all look around. "Hi, Mom."

"Fisher!" Maggie cried delightedly. "Have you come for dinner?"

"No, just a visit. I'm on my way to make a delivery, and then I've got to get back to the ASPCA center." He was holding a parcel.

Maggie took his arm. "Now you listen to me, boy. You've got to eat right. I know you — having a bite of this here and a bite of that there. Well, it's not good enough. Where are you getting your vitamins? Huh?"

"Mom, I'm — "

"No. You need fattening up. You're too thin and that's bad. You come on in and we'll fix you something good. And you can take some banana brownies home with you."

"Mom, I have to take these calcium pills to Paul Channing. His cat's just had kittens and — "

"We could deliver them for you, if you want," Tristan interrupted, pushing his chair back.

Fisher paused for a moment. "Really?" he asked.

"Sure. We don't have much else planned for today."

Andi and Natalie looked at each other, baffled. They had smoothies to finish, and Lola to find. They'd never been so busy! What on earth was Tristan thinking?

Chapter Eight

Tristan held out his hand for the package. "It'll save you having to go all the way over there if we deliver it for you," he said persuasively.

"Well, if you're sure . . . " Fisher handed him the parcel. "You'll have to take it to Mr. Channing's office, though. It's too big to go in his home mailbox. He works at Trantor Insurance in Market Square."

Now Andi knew exactly why Tristan had offered to deliver the pills — he wanted to find out where Mr. Channing worked! And he'd gotten lucky! Giving Natalie a swift kick under the table, she drained her glass and stood up.

"Nice job, Tristan," Natalie said when they were out of earshot. "Now we'll be able to try out Dean's plan and take Mr. Channing's route home."

"We'd better run," Andi said. "It'll be dark soon." She sped up, and Buddy raced along beside her.

"Hang on! Slow down!" Tristan called, running after her.

Andi slowed down to let them catch up, though she was eager to start the search. The light was fading fast now and she hated to think that they might have to wait until tomorrow.

"That's just great!" groaned Tristan as he and Natalie reached her.

"What's up?" Andi asked.

"We passed my mom and dad's real estate office, and my dad was looking out the window."

"What's wrong with that?" Andi was mystified.

"He gave Tristan a thumbs-up," Natalie chuckled. "I bet he was overjoyed to see you getting a little exercise, Tris."

Buddy barked. "I think he's telling us to get a move on," Andi said. "Come on. If we don't hurry, it'll be too dark to see a thing between Market Square and Windrush Drive. Lola could be sitting on the sidewalk under our feet and we wouldn't notice." She glanced up at the sky and her heart sank. It was charcoal gray now, with only a narrow band of brightness in the western sky. "It's too late," she sighed. "We'll have to search tomorrow."

They all fell silent, thinking of poor Lola having to spend another night in a strange place.

"Come on," Natalie said. "We can't stand here all night feeling miserable. We've got to deliver these pills."

They ran again, but this time Andi slowed her pace to match Tristan's and Natalie's.

When they reached Market Square, Tristan looked up at the tall office building and made a face. "I bet he works on the top floor."

"There'd better be an elevator," Natalie puffed. "I've had more than enough exercise for one day."

"I'll take the pills in," Andi said, "while you two catch your breath." She handed Buddy's leash to Natalie and sprinted up the steps to the revolving door.

After leaving the package with the receptionist, she went outside again to find Tristan and Natalie slumped on the steps as if they'd just finished the Boston Marathon. "All done," she said. "I guess we might as well go home."

"What will we be looking for tomorrow, exactly?" Natalie asked.

"A hiding place for a cat," Andi replied. "A garden shed, maybe, that Lola could have gotten shut in. Or a tree she might be stuck in. We have to think about what she might have done if she'd found herself lost outside and gotten scared."

"We'll need a street map," Tristan suggested. "I don't know the business part of Orchard Park that well."

Natalie stood up and smoothed creases from her jeans. "We'll find Lola tomorrow. I'm sure of it."

"I hope you're right," Andi said, crossing her fingers inside the pocket of her jacket, "for Lola's sake."

Tristan and Natalie were waiting for Andi when she arrived in Market Square the next day after school. She'd run home to get Buddy.

"Where's Jet, Natalie?" she asked.

"You know what he's like around cats. He'd probably scare Lola away if he spotted her." Natalie patted Buddy. "Not like you, Bud. You know how to behave."

"*Most* of the time," Andi laughed. "Though, actually, he's pretty bad when it comes to cats. But I'll hold his leash tightly so he can't get near Lola — if we find her." She looked around. "Which way, Tristan?"

"Follow me," he said, unfolding his map.

They started off across the business district of Orchard Park, where there were no yards and the few trees around were too small and spindly to hide a cat, but they peered hopefully under parked cars as they went by.

After about half a mile, the offices gave way to apartment buildings and houses. They were crammed close together, with narrow strips of yard in between.

Suddenly, Buddy started straining against his leash. "Do you think he can smell Lola?" Tristan asked excitedly.

They hurried forward, letting Buddy guide them. He sprang over a low wall and into the narrow garden of an apartment block, nearly pulling Andi's arm out of its socket. Tristan and Natalie scrambled after them.

"It looks like he's really onto something," Tristan panted, as Buddy dove into a clump of bushes.

Andi pushed her way after him, wincing as brambles scratched against her face. *Bud had better be on the trail of something worthwhile*, she thought. The bushes were so thick, she couldn't even see Buddy on the end of the leash.

Suddenly, the leash went slack, and Andi stopped before she stepped on her dog by mistake.

"What did he find?" Natalie called. "Is it Lola?"

Holding her breath, Andi pushed aside some leaves, and found Buddy rooting excitedly under the lid of a discarded pizza box. Her shoulders slumped. "Just an

old pizza box." She pulled Buddy back. "Leave it, Bud."

"What a pain!" Tristan grumbled when they were back on the sidewalk.

They crossed and recrossed the street so they could look on both sides. As they approached Windrush Drive, they walked slower. Andi's spirits sank with every step. They'd soon be at Mr. Channing's house, and if they didn't find any clues to Lola's disappearance in the next few yards, they'd be out of luck. This could turn out to be the first case they wouldn't solve. Andi bit her lip as she remembered how easy finding one pregnant cat had sounded at first.

"What a waste of time," Tristan sighed, echoing her gloomy thoughts. "Trust Dean to come up with a use-less idea."

"It might have worked," Natalie said loyally, turning red.

"But it didn't. So what now?"

"I don't know," Andi replied heavily. She couldn't bear to think about giving up — not when Ms. Giacomo was relying on them. And not when poor Lola was out there somewhere, lost, frightened, and pregnant. But what else could they do? They couldn't scour every street in Orchard Park, hoping to pass by an area that Mr. Channing had.

Dejectedly, they turned onto Windrush Drive and halted outside Mr. Channing's house. "That's that, then," Tristan said, sitting on the wall around the yard. "I'm stumped."

"We can't give up," Natalie said. "We've got to keep looking."

"Jogging!" Andi exclaimed.

Tristan and Natalie stared at her. "You want to go jogging now?" Tristan asked in astonishment. "Do you ever quit?"

"Not me. Mr. Channing. I think he goes jogging. I just remembered I saw his running shoes and gym bag in the hall when we went to see the kittens."

"So?"

"So, maybe he saw Lola when he was jogging. If he has a regular route, we could follow him. Let's come back early tomorrow morning and see where he goes."

"How do you know he goes jogging in the *mornings*?" Tristan asked.

"I don't, but it's worth a try."

Natalie shuddered. "No way am I getting out of bed early in the morning to go jogging!"

"You'll come, won't you, Tris?" Andi asked.

Tristan frowned. "How early are we talking?"

"Six thirty?"

"Six thirty!" He leaped off the wall. "Nobody gets up at six thirty for exercise!"

"Actually, a lot of people do. Say you'll come. I don't want to follow him on my own."

"Six thirty," Tristan groaned, "is the middle of the night."

"Please, Tris. It'll be worth it if it leads us to Lola. You said yourself Ms. Giacomo is depending on us."

He frowned, then nodded reluctantly. "Okay. But don't anyone tell my dad what I'm up to. I don't want him thinking I've turned into a fitness freak."

It was bitterly cold the next morning when Andi slipped out of the house. She ran extra fast to keep warm, and by six twenty she was turning onto Windrush Drive. The houses were dark and the streetlights were still on, but above the mountains the sky was brightening.

Tristan arrived soon after. "You made it," Andi said, grinning. He looked half asleep.

"Don't speak," he groaned. "It's too early for conversation."

They sat on a garden wall and waited for Mr. Channing to come out of his house. There was no sign of life in the Channings' house and Andi began to wonder if she'd gotten it wrong. Maybe Mr. Channing wasn't a morning jogger, after all.

It was nearly seven o'clock when the landing light suddenly went on in his house. "This could be it," Andi whispered.

The front door opened. "There he is!" Andi leaped back behind some branches that overhung the sidewalk. She pulled Tristan after her.

As they'd hoped, Mr. Channing came out of the house dressed in running gear. He jogged straight down his driveway and then along the sidewalk away from them.

"Come on." Andi began to run after him.

"Can't I just wait for you here?" Tristan muttered.

"No! Come on!"

Tristan sprinted to catch up with her. "I hope he doesn't go far," he panted.

Mr. Channing reached the end of the road and turned right. Andi and Tristan followed at a safe distance. As they passed Tangletree House, Andi looked down at the sidewalk. She was glad Tristan was with her, though he was puffing so hard she couldn't imagine him being much help if a ghost suddenly materialized.

They rounded the corner just in time to see Mr. Channing turning right again. "Looks like he's only going around the block," Andi said, disappointed. They'd already searched this area thoroughly.

"Thank goodness," Tristan puffed. "I can't keep going much longer."

As they reached the next corner, they stopped dead in dismay. Mr. Channing was waiting for them, looking very upset. "You again!" he said fiercely. "Are you following me?"

Andi and Tristan stopped, shocked. "N-no," Andi stuttered. "We're searching for Ms. Giacomo's cat, that's all."

"At *this* time of day?"

"At *any* time of day," Tristan puffed, standing his ground. "Lola's pregnant. We have to find her quickly."

"Pregnant?" Mr. Channing's jaw dropped. "I didn't know! Helen never mentioned that."

"That's why we're searching so hard," Andi told him.

Mr. Channing nodded. "Yes, yes. I see. I suppose this does change things." He smiled halfheartedly.

"What does it change?" Tristan demanded.

"Oh, no, nothing. I just understand the urgency now," replied Mr. Channing nervously. "Well, I hope you find her soon." He turned quickly and jogged away.

"Whoa," Andi said when he was out of earshot. "That

was scary." She grinned at Tristan. "You were great, Tris. I'm glad you were here."

"Thanks." He glanced at his watch. "I guess you were right about him only jogging around the block. If he went any farther, he'd be late for work."

"So if he did see Lola when he was jogging, it must have been around here. Maybe we missed something when we were looking before."

"Let's come back after school and take another look," Tristan suggested.

"Okay."

"That's if my legs haven't fallen off," Tristan added, sinking down to sit in a yard. "I don't suppose you'd give me a piggyback ride home, would you?"

Andi laughed. "No way!"

The Pet Finders hurried down to Windrush Drive after school. But, even though they'd gotten out of class as quickly as they could, and Andi had persuaded Tristan and Natalie to jog most of the way to her house to grab Buddy, an early autumn dusk was already settling over the rooftops. The mountains on the horizon seemed to have sucked the light out of the sky, leaving only a pale creamy strip at the edge of dark gray clouds. It was much darker than Andi would have liked for exploring a house with so many haunting legends surrounding it.

"Do you think we'll find anything?" Natalie asked as they stopped on the corner. "We were pretty thorough before."

Andi shrugged. "We've got to do something, and this is the only lead we've got."

They set off along the sidewalk. Tangletree House lay ahead of them, crouching beside the construction site like a sleeping giant. A cold shiver ran down Andi's spine. The boarded-up windows made her nervous. She couldn't help wondering if someone — or something — was hidden behind them, watching their every move through the narrow gaps between the wall planks.

As they passed the old site, they heard a muffled cry.

"What was that?" Natalie gasped, clutching Andi's arm.

The hairs on the back of Andi's neck prickled once again. "I don't know."

They stood still, listening hard over the thudding of their hearts.

"Help!" called a panic-stricken voice. "Help us!"

"Well, that didn't sound like a ghost," said Tristan.

The Pet Finders ran to the chain-link fence in front of the house and peered through. There was nothing to see except the house, the stretch of cleared, muddy ground in front of it where new pipes were being laid, and the line of tangled shrubs and trees still growing beside it. Through the shrubs, they could just make out the main building site with its yawning holes, half-built walls, and bulldozers.

"Who's there?" Tristan called.

"Hello? Anyone? Help!" The voice was coming from beyond the shrubs.

"Don't answer, Tris," Natalie hissed.

"Uh, you don't believe in ghosts," Andi reminded her.

"D-d-didn't," Natalie corrected through chattering teeth. "But you saw the way the dogs behaved last time we were here. And all those people at school believe they've seen or heard something, too. Maybe I was wrong."

"But it doesn't *sound* like a ghost," Tristan insisted moving along the sidewalk in the direction of the voice.

The voice came again. "Please help! We've fallen into a hole!"

"Well, that's either the most cunning ghost I've ever heard of, or some kids have just gotten trapped," said Tristan. He dumped his backpack on the ground and pushed up his sleeves. "Come on, we'll have to get them out."

"What if the ghost comes while we're in there?" Natalie said with a quivering voice. "Maybe they fell into the hole when they were running away from it!"

Andi tried not to listen. She wanted to run away, too.

"We can't leave them," Tristan insisted. He tried to climb up the fence, but the holes in the mesh were too small for his sneakers.

"We're not allowed in there," Andi warned him. "You heard what Ms. Ashworthy and Mr. Dixon said."

"But it's an emergency," Tristan said. "The teachers only meant nobody should go inside to play around."

"It's a shame those guys in there didn't listen," Natalie said sharply. Sighing, she pulled out her cell phone. "I'll call the police, and they'll come pull them out."

"No! Then these kids will get into big trouble," Tristan pointed out.

"Tris is right," Andi agreed. "We should help them ourselves. But we'll have to be careful." She glanced across at Tangletree House, wishing she was anywhere but there.

They searched along the fence for a way in. "Over here," Tristan called, finding a place where the wire had come away from its post. "This must be where they got in."

With trembling hands, Natalie bent the mesh back to

make the gap as wide as possible. She looked down at her jeans, which were streaked with rust, and shrugged. "I guess they just look old-old now, not designer-old."

Andi squeezed Natalie's arm. She could tell her friend was genuinely scared to go onto the site. "We'll be all right in there," she said, trying to reassure herself as much as Natalie. She handed Buddy's leash to Tristan, and then, taking a deep breath, crawled through the gap.

Standing up, Andi looked around. Long dark holes were yawning out of the ground just a few feet away. Beyond them stood half-built brick walls. To her left, partially hidden behind the tangle of shrubs, Tangletree House loomed over them.

Buddy began to whine. "It's okay, Bud," Andi told him. "You can come, too." She reached through the hole and took his leash from Tristan. He scampered through the gap, then jumped up at her, clearly relieved that they were together again.

Natalie and Tristan crawled through. Natalie frowned at the churned-up earth in front of them. "Do we really have to tromp through this?"

"Looks like it," Tristan said, sounding as if he was making a huge effort to stay cheerful.

Andi began to feel a little better. There were three of them, after all, and they had Buddy with them. "Come on," she said. "We'd better find those kids quickly, since we're not even supposed to *be* here." She raised her voice. "Where are you guys?" she called.

"Over here!"

"Keep yelling so we know which direction to take."

They moved forward, following the sound of a boy's voice and trying to move around the worst of the mud. The ground had been so badly upturned by bulldozers and dump trucks that their sneakers were soon thickly caked and felt like they weighed twenty times more than usual.

"This is horrible!" Natalie said.

"That's construction sites for you," Tristan pointed out.

"I don't just mean the mud. I mean everything." She meant the ghost that was supposed to haunt Tangletree House.

Andi squelched along through the mud, keeping her gaze fixed on the ground. She was determined not to look at the old house. "There's no such thing as ghosts," she muttered under her breath. "There's no such thing as ghosts." If only she could convince herself it was true . . .

Chapter Nine

"Where are you?" the boy called. He sounded much closer now. "Hurry up!"

"We're almost there!" Tristan called back. "The hole must be really deep," he added in a low voice. "I can't see them at all. I hope we can get them out."

"Me, too," Andi agreed grimly.

Struggling to keep their footing in the slippery mud, the Pet Finders skirted around a huge stack of bricks. Passing two mud-spattered bulldozers, they found themselves on the edge of a trench that was longer and deeper than all the others. Andi held Buddy's leash tightly, afraid that he might fall in.

"At least those guys had a soft landing, with all this mud," Tristan muttered.

"True," Andi agreed.

Suddenly, her foot slipped. For a moment, she teetered on the very edge of the trench, flapping her arms in a desperate attempt to keep her balance. Below her, she could see three mud-plastered figures, one sitting and two standing. They were gazing up at her, open-mouthed with dismay.

"Andi!" Tristan yelled. He grabbed her around the waist and jerked her back from the edge.

Andi let out a long, shuddering breath. "Thanks, Tris," she gasped. "That was close."

"Are you all right?" Natalie asked, concerned.

Andi nodded. She was shaken, but she wasn't hurt. And at least they'd found the kids.

The hole was about twelve feet deep. "Can you get us out?" called one of the boys. He was tall and broad-shouldered and wore a muddy, hooded top. "Kenny and I are okay, but Brad hurt his ankle." He pointed to a thin boy with spiky hair who was sitting in the mud, clutching his ankle.

"We're going to need a rope," said Tristan.

"Maybe there'll be one under here," Andi suggested, spotting a lumpy tarpaulin nearby. She heaved up the edge to discover an untidy heap of buckets, shovels, pickaxes, bags of cement, boxes of nails, and rolls of roofing felt. Andi searched through the heap, then gave a triumphant shout. "Got one!" Miraculously, there was a rope coiled neatly inside one of the buckets. It looked thick enough to hold her weight, and she felt a sudden surge of assurance.

Dragging the rope out from under the tarpaulin, Andi tied one end around the trunk of a nearby tree and lowered the other end into the hole. "Hold on," she called down to the boys. "I'll come down and give you a hand."

"Be careful, Andi," Tristan warned.

"I'll be fine," Andi told him, trying to ignore the lump in her throat. It suddenly looked a very long way down to the bottom of the hole. She handed Buddy's leash to Natalie. "Stay, Bud," she commanded.

Buddy gazed up at her miserably. He hated being left behind.

"It's all right, boy. I'll be quick," Andi promised. She wiped her muddy hands on her sweatshirt before grabbing hold of the rope. Taking a deep breath, she swung herself over the edge of the pit. Natalie and Tristan watched her anxiously.

"I thought we were supposed to be saving pets, not people," Andi called up to them, trying to ease the tension. Natalie smiled weakly and Tristan managed a half-hearted laugh.

Andi knew she had reached the bottom of the rope when she sank up to her ankles in mud. "Yuck!" she groaned.

Two of the boys waded across to her. "That was some climb," one of them said, impressed. "I'm Carl."

"Andi. Can you climb up there?" she asked.

"Sure. Kenny, hold the rope tight for me." Carl began to haul himself up the rope, grunting and puffing with effort.

Andi crouched beside Brad. His ankle was bruised and swollen. "That looks pretty bad," she said sympathetically.

"Yeah. I won't be able to climb that rope."

"The others will have to pull you up." Andi glanced around. Carl had reached the top of the rope and was standing on the edge of the pit with Tristan and Natalie. "Come on, Kenny," he called. "Get a move on."

Kenny was dangling a few feet off the ground. "Can you hold the rope still for me?" he panted, looking at Andi. "I can't get a grip with it swinging around like this."

Andi seized the end of the rope and held it taut.

"Thanks." Kenny began to climb. Slowly, he inched his way up, red-faced with effort and his arms shaking with weight and tension. When he was almost to the top, he started slipping down again. "Help!" he yelled.

Tristan let go of the rope and reached down to him. "Grab my hand. I'll pull you up."

"I can't," Kenny wailed, sliding down another few inches.

Tristan and Carl knelt in the mud and leaned over as far as they could. "Come on!" Tristan called. "You can do it."

Kenny looked up at him despairingly, then made a lunge for his hand. Tristan caught him by the wrist, Carl caught his other hand, and together they hauled him up out of sight from Andi and Brad, who waited at the bottom of the hole.

"I'm going to tie the rope around Brad," Andi called. "You'll have to pull him up, then drop the rope down to me again so I can climb out." She hauled Brad to his feet, then helped him hobble to the side of the pit.

"Okay!" she called. "He's ready."

Natalie held Buddy's leash while Tristan, Kenny, and Carl seized the rope. They began to pull.

Brad was lifted off his feet. He dangled for a moment, turning slowly like a broken puppet, then began to rise jerkily into the air.

In a few long moments, he'd reached the top. He sank down to the ground, moaning and clutching his injured ankle. Tristan then untied the rope and dropped it down to Andi.

"Thanks," she said. She wiped her hands on her jeans to remove the worst of the mud, then swung herself easily up the rope.

Buddy started barking madly as she emerged from the hole. The moment she landed, he leaped up onto her, making her jeans muddier than ever.

"It's okay, Bud," Andi said. "I'm back now, though I don't know how I'm going to explain all this mud to Mom. . . ." She shrugged. "Oh, well, at least we've got our new washing machine."

"That was amazing, Andi," said Tristan as they coiled the rope and put it back under the tarpaulin. "Where did you learn to climb like that?"

Andi shrugged. "Back in Florida. I always loved gym classes."

"It shows," Tristan told her. "I've never seen anyone climb like that. Except monkeys, of course," he added with a grin.

Andi aimed a playful slap at him, which he dodged.

"What were you doing on the building site?" Natalie asked the boys.

Carl looked down at his feet. "Ghost hunting."

"We didn't believe there was a ghost," Kenny added. "Not really." His eyes stretched wide with fear. "Until we heard it."

"It was wailing," Carl said shakily. "So we ran for it. That was how we fell down that hole."

"I knew it," Natalie muttered to Andi. "Let's get out of here."

Kenny and Carl supported Brad as they headed for the gap in the fence. Andi, Tristan, and Natalie followed with Buddy.

"How's Brad going to get through the hole in the fence?" Natalie asked. "He can't put any weight on that ankle."

"We'll have to go out the main gate," said Carl. "The one right in front of the house." He didn't need to say what was on everyone's mind: This would mean going much closer to the haunted ruin.

Natalie leaned close to Andi. "Buddy will protect us if we see anything, won't he?" she whispered.

"We won't see anything," Andi replied, hoping that she was right.

They reached the tangle of shrubs that grew beside Tangletree House. "We'll have to go between these bushes and the house wall," Tristan said. "It's the only way to reach the main gate."

Fearfully, Andi looked up at the house. It seemed bigger and spookier than ever, and it was all too easy to imagine a whole army of ghosts inside, just waiting for

the right moment to drift through the walls and sur-
round them.

They set off along the narrow path, moving as quietly
as they could. Low branches snatched at their clothes
with thorny fingers, and Andi's hair stood on end every
time something brushed against her face.

"Oh, this is hopeless!" Natalie groaned, stopping to
untangle her sleeve from another bramble. "We'll never
get out of here at this rate. . . ."

Just then, her words were drowned out by a hideous,
shrieking, ghostly wail.

Chapter Ten

"It's the ghost!" Carl yelled.

"Let's get out of here!" Kenny wailed. He and Carl let go of Brad and sprinted off around the front of the house.

Brad dropped to the ground with a cry of pain. "My ankle!"

Andi's heart leaped into her throat and stayed there. Fighting back the fear that told her to get out of there immediately, she ran over and seized Brad's arm. "Help me get him up, Nat!" she said breathlessly. "We can't leave him here."

Natalie grabbed Brad's other arm and they hauled him to his feet. Then, half carrying, half dragging, they moved him along the path. Twigs and thorns snagged painfully in Andi's hair as she stumbled along. What if the ghost appeared now? They'd never outrun it with Brad slowing them down.

They reached the corner of the house. The gate leading to the street stood open about thirty feet away. There was no sign of Carl or Kenny.

Andi and Natalie headed for the gate, with Buddy scampering beside them. "Nearly there," Andi gasped. She looked back, expecting to see Tristan hard on their heels. But he was standing beside the front porch of the haunted house, staring at a boarded-up window.

"Tristan!" Andi yelled. "Come on! We've got to go!"

He didn't move.

"Tristan!" she cried again.

"He must have seen the ghost!" Natalie said hoarsely. "He's too scared to move. We'll have to go back for him."

They sat Brad down on a tree stump and darted back. "Wait!" he called after them. "Don't leave me!"

"We've got to help Tristan!" Natalie puffed. "We'll come back for you in a minute."

Andi reached Tristan first. She grabbed his arm and tried to pull him away. "Tristan! You've got to come."

"No, wait." He shook her off. "Look at the window."

Andi looked at it fearfully, expecting to see a pair of

evil eyes peering through a crack, but there was nothing to see except planks nailed across the gap where glass used to be. "What?" she asked.

"That plank's been moved." Sure enough, one of the planks had slid down a little, leaving a narrow opening.

"So?" Andi was feeling a little less scared now — it was hard to stay spooked with Tristan pointing out gaps in planks.

Natalie reached them. "Come on, Tristan," she said in a shaky voice.

"But why would a ghost move a plank? Ghosts can walk through walls." Tristan looked at Andi and Natalie, his eyes thoughtful. "That plank was definitely nailed across the window when I came past here on Wednesday morning. I was helping Dean with his paper route, and we were joking about the number of papers he'd have to deliver when all this building work's finished. We counted the windows to see if we could figure out how many apartments there'll be, and there was no gap then."

"How can you be so sure?" Natalie pressed.

"I just am. I remember things like that. You know, like the Sun-Ripe number on that truck."

Suddenly, Buddy gave a loud whine and jerked on his leash.

The Pet Finders nearly jumped out of their skins. Andi groaned, getting ready to run as if all the soccer tryouts in the world depended on it.

"No, wait!" Tristan cried. "Look, Buddy's pulling *toward* the house, not *away* from it. He wants to go inside!"

It was true. Buddy was straining toward the house. And he didn't seem at all frightened. His ears were pricked up, and his tail was wagging.

"I want a closer look at that plank," Tristan continued. He swallowed hard. "Will you come with me?"

Andi's stomach lurched, but she could see that Tristan wasn't going anywhere until he'd investigated properly, and they couldn't leave him on his own. "Okay," she agreed.

"What are you doing?" Brad called. "Don't leave me!"

"We won't be long," Andi promised.

They walked up the steps of the porch, then crept along it, carefully avoiding the rotten planks. When they were almost to the window, the eerie wail sang out, freezing them in their tracks.

But if Andi was being honest with herself, Buddy still didn't look the least bit scared. If anything, he seemed excited.

As the unearthly sound died away, Tristan spoke in a

low voice: "Come on. We still need to look at that window."

"Don't, Tristan," Natalie whimpered. "Let's get out of here."

"No, wait," Andi urged. "If Tristan's onto something, we should investigate."

"We're the *Pet* Finders, remember?" Natalie said. "That means we should be investigating pets, right? Not ghosts."

"Come on," Tristan said. "It'll be all right."

They tiptoed forward again. In a few steps, they reached the window and gathered around it, trembling.

"There!" Tristan hissed. "What's that you were saying, Nat?" A small bunch of blue-gray hairs were clinging to rough edges of the window frame. "I think we might have found a missing pet after all!"

"Lola," they all whispered together.

"This must be where Mr. Channing saw her. He jogged right by here, even if it *is* just around his own block." Andi licked her dry lips. "We'll have to go in and look for her."

"What about the ghost?" Natalie cringed.

"There is no ghost," Andi said. She suddenly realized that there had been something rather familiar about the wailing that had spooked them so much. "I think all that yowling was Lola, trying to get out."

"But Larissa's cousin — or friend — or whoever — *saw* something."

"Maybe he imagined it. Maybe he heard Lola and was frightened by a shadow or something."

"And what if he didn't imagine it?" Natalie persisted. "What if there *is* a ghost inside? The legends about this place are much older than Lola's disappearance."

Andi rubbed her hands together, trying to stop them from trembling. She couldn't tell Natalie absolutely that there weren't any ghosts inside the house, however logical she made it sound. "There's only one way to find out."

They tiptoed back along the porch to the front door.

"What are you doing *now*?" Brad called, as Tristan opened the door a crack.

"We'll be as quick as we can!" Tristan promised. He pressed his eye to the crack. "I can't see anything."

"At least leave me your dog for protection!" Brad begged. "I don't want to be by myself!"

The Pet Finders looked at one another. "I suppose we could leave Buddy out here," Andi said. "It'll keep him from trying to chase Lola when we find her."

"*If* we find her," Natalie said.

Andi led the little dog over to Brad. "Stay, Bud," she said, patting him.

"Thanks." Brad looked a little happier as he leaned up against Buddy. "I'll watch him. Don't worry."

Andi ran back to the others. "Let's go."

Natalie looked back at her with huge, anxious eyes. "Look, guys, do you really think this is a good idea? We're going to get in a lot more trouble for going inside the house than we are for just being in the yard."

Tristan rolled his eyes. "How can we call ourselves Pet Finders if we don't even try looking?" he asked impatiently. He put his shoulder against the door and braced himself to give it a shove.

Wham! The door flew open and crashed back against the inside wall, sending Tristan staggering into the hallway with his arms flailing. Andi bit her lip to stop a nervous giggle from bursting out.

Tristan dusted his hands off, annoyed. "Well, are you coming in?" he demanded.

Andi glanced at Natalie and nodded. Taking a deep breath, they stepped through the old door frame, and followed Tristan into the house.

As soon as they shuffled through the door, it swung

shut behind them, plunging them into gloomy darkness. The only light came from the narrow gaps between the planks covering the windows. For a moment, Andi couldn't see a thing. The lump in her throat was back, and she was convinced that someone — some*thing* — was about to grab her. Then her eyes grew accustomed to the dimness, and she saw that they were in an enormous entrance hall. Muddy boot trails led across the floor to a broad flight of stairs with ornate wooden banisters. Somehow it didn't seem quite as scary, knowing that the construction workers had been in here already.

"Which way?" Natalie breathed.

Andi looked around uncertainly. The old house was massive. It would take them forever to search every room.

Suddenly, the shrill wail sounded again, louder than ever.

Even though she told herself again and again that the unearthly sound *was* Lola, Andi's heart flipped over and her hands got clammy. She wished that she'd brought Buddy inside after all. It would have been reassuring to feel his warmth against her leg. But there was no time to go back and get him — Lola needed to be rescued, and fast.

"That came from upstairs," she said, sounding much braver than she felt. She led the way to the stairs and started to climb. Each step creaked under their feet, as if they were walking through the set of an old horror movie. Andi resisted the urge to giggle out loud.

At the top of the stairs, a long landing stretched away in both directions. Which way now?

"Lola!" Andi called. "Where are you, girl?" Her voice echoed along the corridor.

There was an answering wail. Now that they could hear it clearly, it was definitely a cat in distress.

"Down there!" Natalie said, sounding much less frightened now.

They sped along the landing, following Lola's cry. Racing through a half-open door, they found themselves in a bathroom. Shining silver faucets gleamed in the twilight, above a bathtub that was fit snugly inside a base of beautiful, dark, wooden panels. The builders must have just finished work in there.

"Lola!" Andi called again. "Where are you, sweetheart?"

A dismal howl came from behind one of the panels alongside the bath. Andi flung herself down beside it and pressed her eye to a crack. A pair of glittering eyes looked back at her, like green flames in the darkness. Andi lurched back. "It's those eyes!" she croaked.

"What? What is it?" Natalie demanded, backing away from the tub.

Cautiously, Andi peered through the crack again. The eyes were still there and the wail sounded again. "They're Lola's eyes!" Andi exclaimed.

As Lola's wail died away, she heard a chorus of tiny yelps.

"So you can see her?" Tristan asked.

"Yes! And I think she's had her kittens!"

Chapter Eleven

"Help me get this panel off," Andi said. She tried to squeeze her fingers into a miniscule gap between the wooden panels, so that she could lever one of them off, but it was too narrow.

"Try lifting it from the bottom," Tristan suggested, crouching beside her. Natalie kneeled at the far end and they pulled together, but the panel wouldn't budge.

"The builders must have screwed it in place," Andi groaned.

They searched frantically for a screwdriver, but the workers hadn't left any tools behind.

"Poor Lola," Andi said desperately. "She must have been cooped up in there for days. We've got to get her out fast."

But the wooden panel stayed put.

"Give me your phone, Natalie!" Tristan said suddenly.

"Who are you calling?" Andi asked.

"The fire department. And then I'll call Fisher so he can come check Lola and her kittens."

Andi crouched beside the bathtub. "It's okay, girl," she told the frightened cat. "We're going to get you out of there." She couldn't see or hear Lola anymore, but she could hear the occasional faint meow from the kittens. "Ms. Giacomo's going to be so happy we found you."

The firefighters arrived in a truck with its siren blaring and red lights flashing. Tristan went to meet them, and Andi listened to Lola's rescuers pounding up the stairs.

"She's trapped behind those panels," Andi said, pointing to the bathtub, when the men appeared in the doorway, looking reassuring in their broad-shouldered yellow fire gear.

"Stand back," said one of them, heaving a toolbox into the tiny room.

Andi and Natalie scrambled up and squeezed into the far corner. Andi had pins and needles from crouching down for so long, and she shook each foot in turn as the firemen began to remove the panel.

They heard more footsteps on the landing, and then a stocky, dark-haired man appeared. "What's going on?" he demanded.

"A cat's trapped behind the bathtub panels," Tristan explained.

"Trapped? It can't be. My workers put that tub in days ago. There's no way a cat could have gotten behind there since then. They always do a good job."

"She must have slipped in while they were installing it," Andi said. "Maybe when they stopped for a break. Then when they put the panel in place, she was trapped."

The builder pushed back his baseball hat and scratched his head. "And she's been in there all this time? Poor thing. I guess we'd never have heard her during the day — this is a pretty noisy place when the guys are working."

There was a loud cracking sound as one of the firemen used a screwdriver to pry at the wooden panel, and the builder frowned. "Hey, be careful! This is a top-of-the-line bathtub unit!"

Andi opened her mouth to protest that Lola and her kittens were much more important than any bathroom unit, but she caught Natalie giving her a warning glance and quickly stopped. There was another creak that made the builder wince, and then a loud snapping sound. The two firemen stepped away carrying the panel between them, and there was Lola, crouched protectively in front of three tiny, fluffy kittens. Her fur was covered in dust and grime, and she was blinking hard in the sudden burst of light, but she was obviously determined to be a great mother to her little family.

"Oh, Lola!" Andi whispered. "I can't believe we found you!"

"What do you know!" said the builder. "The guys aren't gonna believe me when I tell them about this."

Tristan gently lifted Lola up. He turned on the tub faucet and let cold water run into his hand. Lola lapped thirstily, then snuggled down in his arms as if she knew he'd come to rescue her.

Andi scooped up two of the kittens and held them against her chest. Their eyes were shut tightly in the bright light, and their tiny tails stuck up in the air.

"Oh, they're so sweet!" Natalie exclaimed, as she picked up the last kitten. They were soft and warm, and began to purr in tiny, rumbling voices as the girls cradled them.

The firemen crowded around to pet the cats, their hands giant and clumsy in their protective gloves.

"Lucky you kids found them," said the one who had carried the tools.

Suddenly, they heard Fisher's voice. "Hello? Is anyone here?"

"In here!" Tristan called back.

Fisher came into the bathroom. "You've found your missing Russian Blue," he said, beaming at them. "Good work! Let me see her." He pulled out his stethoscope and listened to Lola's chest. Then he checked her ears and eyes. "How long do you think she's been shut in?"

"Ms. Giacomo said she disappeared nearly a week ago," Tristan replied.

Fisher smiled. "You'd never know it. She's in perfect health." He scratched Lola's ears, and she rubbed her head against his hand. "I guess she's been catching mice to keep her strength up." He checked the kittens one by one. "And there's nothing wrong with these beauties, either. You guys did a great job tracking them down!"

"Thanks!" said Andi. She grinned at Natalie and Tristan.

"We'd better go," Natalie said. "We don't want to keep Ms. Giacomo waiting."

They carried Lola and her kittens downstairs. As

they came outside, they saw a policeman speaking to Carl, Kenny, and Brad. "All the schools in the area have warned children to keep off this construction site," he said sternly. "So what on earth were you doing in here?"

The three boys hung their heads. "We were only wandering around," Carl muttered.

"Hey, Gerry," one of the firemen called to the policeman.

The policeman glanced around. "Hi, Tim. I saw your engine and came to see if I could help. Then I spotted these three. Two of them had come back to look for their friend, who hurt his ankle falling into a pit." He gave an exaggerated sigh. "Honestly, can't kids see the danger in playing on construction sites?"

Buddy spotted Andi and jumped up, barking a greeting. "Do you think you can hold all three kittens, Natalie?" Andi asked. "I think Buddy's feeling a bit jealous."

"Sure I can," Natalie said. Her voice had gone all dreamy, like when she was looking at Snowdrop's kittens.

The policeman caught sight of the Pet Finders. "Good grief, more kids! Now you listen to me — "

"They only came to help us!" Carl told him quickly. "They heard us yelling."

"And they've saved the lives of a cat and her kittens," Fisher added.

The policeman's eyebrows shot up. "Is that right? They're neighborhood heroes for trespassing?" He looked back at the fireman, who was quietly shaking his head as if to say that his reaction wasn't necessary. "Oh, all right." The policeman turned back to Carl, Kenny, and Brad. "This time. But I'll be speaking to your school principal about finding you here. And if I ever catch you on a construction site again — "

"You won't," Brad said quickly, rubbing his swollen ankle.

"Definitely not," Kenny and Carl promised.

"Glad to hear it." The policeman headed for his car.

"That ankle looks as though it needs some attention," Fisher said. "Would you guys like a lift home?"

"Yes, please," Brad replied. Kenny and Carl helped him limp over to the gate.

"How far are you going with these cats?" one of the firemen asked.

"Just around the corner," Tristan said. "Scayne Place."

"Want a ride in a fire truck?"

The Pet Finders looked at one another, each clearly thinking the same thing. *"Yes!"* Andi exclaimed.

*   *   *

The fire engine drew up outside Ms. Giacomo's house with a hiss of brakes.

"Thanks for the ride!" Andi said as she leaped down from the cab. Buddy jumped down after her.

Natalie and Tristan climbed down, and the firemen passed Lola and her kittens to them.

"See you guys!" the men called as they drove away.

"Bye! Thanks for everything!"

As the Pet Finders hurried up the path, they saw Mr. Channing standing on the doorstep talking to Ms. Giacomo. He looked agitated. "I know I should have told you before, Helen, but . . . "

"Yes, you should have!" Ms. Giacomo interrupted angrily. "Lola and her kittens could be . . . " Her gaze fell on the Pet Finders. "Lola!" she cried. She ran past Mr. Channing and swept Lola out of Tristan's arms. "Oh, thank you! Thank you!" She hugged her cat tightly.

"Please don't say anything to the show authorities," Mr. Channing pleaded. "It was stupid of me to keep quiet about seeing Princess Anastasia, but I thought it might give one of my cats a chance to win first prize for once. And now you've got her back, so there was no harm done."

"I don't want to talk about this now," Ms. Giacomo

snapped. "Please go away, Paul." She turned her back on him and beamed at the Pet Finders. "Come in, come in!"

"We're a little muddy," Natalie said doubtfully.

"Oh, don't worry about it."

"Helen, please . . . " Mr. Channing called as the Pet Finders followed Ms. Giacomo inside. He tried to follow, but she shut the door firmly.

"Lola had her kittens!" Andi said. "Look."

Ms. Giacomo gave a gasp of delight and spun around to see them. "They're gorgeous," she cooed. "Absolutely beautiful." She sat down with Lola, and Natalie placed the kittens in her lap. "I bet you're wondering why Paul Channing was here," she said, stroking each of the kittens in turn. "It turns out he saw Lola going into Tangletree House last week. Apparently, he didn't tell me before because he wanted his cat, Beauty, to win next week's show."

"So why did he come today?" Natalie asked.

"He heard that Lola was pregnant. He felt bad about her condition, and he knew she couldn't enter the show with young kittens to care for, anyway." She shook her head, clearly still angry. "But I thought we were friends! I should have listened to you kids."

"Will you report him?" Andi asked.

"I don't know. I'll have to think about that." She laughed. "But I definitely won't be sharing my coffee with him at any more cat shows!"

"We still don't know how Lola got out of your house," Tristan said. "I'm thinking it *had* to be that screen door. Do you mind if we take another look at it?"

"Help yourselves," Ms. Giacomo said.

They went into the kitchen. Andi opened the back door, revealing the familiar screen door. They all stared at it for a few moments, but didn't notice anything peculiar. Then Tristan crouched down and put his hand on the bottom of the door.

"Look at this!" Tristan tilted the door. "The bottom hinge is broken. All you have to do is apply a little pressure, and this gap opens up." The space between the door frame and screen was certainly big enough for even a large cat to fit through.

They hurried back to the living room to tell Ms. Giacomo.

"Thank goodness you caught that," she said. "There's no way I would have noticed it, and Lola or Deena might have gotten out again." She gave them a proud smile. "I might need one of you guys to move in here, to keep an eye on us!" she laughed. "Well, maybe not *all* of us. But maybe one of you would like a kitten when they're old enough to leave Lola?"

Andi's heart skipped a beat. The kittens were so sweet! It would be the best thing ever to have one of her own. Then she glanced down at Buddy, who was lying with his head on her feet. Maybe the *second* best thing ever. Nothing could beat having Buddy around. And it had been hard work looking after Apple as well as Buddy, so Andi knew she only had time for one pet. "Not me, thanks," she said. "I've got Buddy."

"And Jet sometimes chases cats," Natalie said wistfully, "so it wouldn't be fair to the kitten."

They turned to look at Tristan. "How about you, Tris?" Andi prompted. "You haven't got a pet."

He looked down at the kittens. "They're great," he agreed. "But I still think Lucy might come home one day. It would be terrible if she turned up and found a new cat had taken her place."

Andi's heart sank with a thud. "Lucy's been gone a long time," she reminded him gently.

"I know, but . . . " He broke off and forced a smile. "No, thanks, Ms. Giacomo."

"Well, you can still come see Lola anytime you like," she told them.

After some cocoa, they finally said their good-byes and headed for home. Andi was very worried about how unhappy Tristan seemed. She wished they could find Lucy for him, but she'd been missing for months. There couldn't possibly be a trail to follow after so long.

"Cheer up, Tris," said Natalie. "The Pet Finders have done it again!"

"It was a great result," Andi agreed. "We started out looking for one lost cat and ended up finding four!"

Tristan nodded. "You're right. There's no point in getting upset." He grinned. "I wonder what animal we'll be searching for next?"

"You never know, we might have to go into *people* finding as well," Andi joked. "We found Apple's owner, and we found Carl, Kenny, and Brad."

"I don't mind finding people," Natalie said firmly, hoisting her backpack onto her shoulder. "Just as long as we *don't* have to find any ghosts!"

ABOUT THE AUTHOR

Ben Baglio was born in New York, and grew up in a small town in southern New Jersey. He was the only boy in a family with three sisters.

Ben spent a lot of his childhood reading. English was always his favorite subject, and after graduating from high school, he went on to study English Literature at the University of Pennsylvania. During his coursework, he was able to spend a year in Edinburgh, Scotland.

After graduation, Ben Baglio worked as a children's book editor in New York City. He also wrote his first book, which was about the Olympics in ancient Greece. Five years later, he took a job at a publishing house in England.

Ben Baglio is the author of the *Dolphin Diaries* series, and is perhaps most well known for the *Animal Ark* and *Animal Ark Hauntings* series. These books were originally published in England (under the pseudonym Lucy Daniels), and have since gone on to be published in the United States and translated into 15 languages.

Aside from writing, Ben enjoys scuba diving and swimming, music and movies. He has a beagle named Bob, who is by his side whenever he writes.